LIVE FOR TODAY

Joe Barfield

CreateSpace Publishing

Live For Today

ISBN:
ISBN-13:978-1484823491

DEDICATION

My wife, Lucia who wanted me to write the story.

Cover Illustration
By
Del Flores

Original edit
By
Kristin McKenzie

Live For Today

A broken promise takes a gifted seventeen-year-old boy down a suicidal path of self-destruction. Will the persistence of his coach and love of a girl be enough to save him?

A Note About *Live For Today*
The Movie

The story of *Live For Today* has been made into a heart-tugging, anti-bullying, faith-based movie. It was filmed with student actors and locals from the Katy, Texas area with a $2,000 Cannon 7D camera—nearly unheard of in the world of feature length films. At this point, we are in the sound editing phase and are pursuing the licensing of music.

YouTube, Facebook, and our production company website bring you current news, movie posters, photos, cast members, author biographies, and fundraising information. Check out the trailer. You will witness a film that rivals a studio quality motion picture.

Browse through our website and see how you can become part of this cause.

www.K-TFilms.com

See the Live For Today Trailer
http://goo.gl/Oesoxd

Live For Today is based, in part, on a true account of tragedy, love and finding the meaning of life. What happened to me in high school left memories, scars and lessons. After all, *Live For Today* is about high school, football and coming of age. Hardships, hope and choices… this is a story—the story—reflected in the halls of every high school campus in the '60s, and today.

Bullying and suicide still plague our campuses as young people struggle to find their own redemption story. This book demonstrates that a path of self-destruction can be shaped into something positive.

Historic snapshots of Houston are embedded in the pages. We played sandlot football across from the Hofheinz mansion right around the time the Astrodome was built. We marveled at the invention of Astroturf. We swam in Buffalo Bayou and cruised Westheimer. We hung out with guys like Billy Gibbons and listened to music from his band, the Moving Sidewalks, which played a key role in our lives. We played football for the

Robert E. Lee High Generals. The pictures in *Live For Today* are from the movie and accompanied by authentic photos from my 1967 Robert E. Lee yearbook.

A crew of Katy ISD students latched on to the screen play. They were determined to make the movie, so we held auditions, picked a cast, and filmed at Surfside Beach and at authentic campuses and athletic fields. The production team still has more to do before we can debut at the Austin Film Festival. With financial help, our goals are achievable. For every book sold, a percentage goes towards final sound editing.

Help us prove that students can make a professional film, and that a big effort from a small town can make a huge impact on the world.

Foreword

By Dene Hofheinz Anton

My Dad, Judge Roy Hofheinz, loved Houston, Texas. Houston and Hofheinz almost became synonymous, and it wasn't just the alliteration. It was Inspiration. Some folks may remember his accomplishments throughout the '40s, '50s, '60s and '70s, perhaps the most remarkable being the construction of the Astrodome (a first) and Astroworld. Daddy was also able to influence his good friend Lyndon B. Johnson into bringing the Space Center to Houston/Harris County.

Thanks to "The Judge" as he liked to be called, Houston became a major sports, entertainment and convention center. The Rev. Billy Graham nicknamed the Astrodome the "Eighth Wonder of the World," and Astroworld provided a healthy and fun-filled environment for youngsters. These ventures created thousands of jobs for Houstonians of all ages. In fact, actor Dennis Quaid's first job was as a clown at Astroworld. Appearances at the Astrodome by the Ringling Brothers and Barnum & Bailey Circus, plus Baseball, Football, the Houston Livestock Show and Rodeo and so many artists and concerts, brought joy to many families. You can just about name it… my father brought it to Houston.

As I read "Live for Today," I was taken back to those earlier decades and reminded of my parents' involvement with the youth of our great city. At the age of 24, Dad became the Harris County Judge and presided over juvenile court. He ordered troubled children to regularly attend church and receive counseling from a minister. These children were also committed to checking in with my patient and nurturing mother. Certainly, this was unorthodox from every angle, but Mama was a Saint and could cure angst of all kinds. Kindly, she made sure that suicidal children receive counseling. Daddy also ordered juvenile delinquents to include art and music in their classes, and to get involved in sports—if not as players, as spectators. In "The Judge's" view, good sportsmanship was a metaphor of life and a key ingredient. Daddy felt that sports kept young 'uns from running wild in the streets, so to speak, by keeping them focused and involved with each other in a common interest. I was touched that the author and his buddies had played sandlot football in the yard of our homestead on Yorktown road in southwest Houston.

For nearly two centuries, families have been attracted to Houston, making it the fourth largest city in the nation. With the influx of families came students, who quickly filled up the schools. The stories of these students are captured in "Live for Today"—stories that my Mom and Dad, who cared so much for young people, would have related to on many levels.

High school antics and youthful indiscretions have always been a part of campus life. But sometimes the teen years pose greater challenges. Peer pressure, bullying and the problems associated with "not fitting in" can be monumental and seemingly insurmountable, causing some to seek a "permanent" and tragic solution to a temporary problem. "Live for Today" addresses the very real threat of teen suicide. In his own high school years, the author personally experienced this loss and seeks to educate and spread awareness in this "coming of age" novel uniquely set in Houston.

Interestingly, Billy Gibbons of The Moving Sidewalks (and later ZZ Top) was a schoolmate of the author and appears in the book. They congregated at the Catacombs and listened to disc jockey Russ Knight (also known as the "Weird Beard") on KILT. The nostalgia runs deep, and the message is eternal...

How fantastic that "Live for Today" has been filmed as a feature-length motion picture. As it debuts at the Austin Film Festival, I'm optimistic that Tribeca and Sundance won't be far behind.

LIVE FOR TODAY

TABLE OF CONTENTS

	Acknowledgments	i
	Miracles	3
1	Summer of '61	7
2	Class of '67	23
3	Houston and New Friends	28
4	Surfside	36
5	Live For Today	40
6	Robert E. Lee Generals	54
7	The Challenge	58
8	Sandlot Wars	62
9	Slumber Party	74
10	Coach Turner Forces a Challenge	77
11	Friday Night Lights	81
12	Coach's Challenge Works	93
13	A Quarterback Threat	99
14	The Catacombs	100
15	Runaround Sue	106
16	Mom	113
17	Ultimatum	115
18	Jim's World Crumbles	110
19	Coach Turner Reveals the Secret	118
20	Another Secret Revealed	120
21	The Fight	121
22	Dawn Learns the Truth	124
23	Turner Gives Lance an Option	125
24	Exposed	127
25	Garner State Park	129
26	The Swing	134
27	Death and the Secret	137
28	The Return	142
	Epilog	147
	AUTHOR'S COMMENTS	150
	ABOUT THE AUTHOR	153
	The 60's Slang	155
	Surfer Slang	163
	Other Books by Joe Barfield	169

ACKNOWLEDGMENTS

Bullies come in all shapes and sizes. I was bullied. It's strange to "thank" a tormentor, but if it had not been for the torment, I would have never lived my journey. This book and movie would have never been born.

Set in Houston and Surfside Beach in the '60s, the social habits of that era fill the pages. The legal drinking age was eighteen. Corporal punishment was alive and well. We had our own vernacular which you'll find in the back of the book. Houston landmarks are featured prominently: Buffalo Bayou, Westheimer, Robert E. Lee High School and the Tanglewood subdivision. The "sandlot" across from the Hofheinz Manson was our default practice field and the groundskeeper didn't mind us playing football as long as Judge Roy Hofheinz was off premises. He was busy launching the Eighth Wonder of the World—The Astrodome.

This book has been made into a feature length motion picture. The professionals said students weren't capable of such a feat. They were wrong. A dedicated group of teens from Katy, Texas, along with actors and crew from in and around west Houston, made a motion picture that moved them to their core. They want to see it in theaters. The goal is to honor their wishes. With your help, we'll launch this project at the Austin Film Festival and beyond.

Special thanks to Kristin McKenzie, who as a first year theatre, Bible and English teacher, worked hard on behalf of this project and took a lead role. The movie was filmed on her parent's land, at Surfside Beach, and in the halls and athletic fields of local campuses. She also edited the original version of *Live For Today* and was instrumental in the filming of the movie.

Thanks to Brian Mathew Carr, who played a lead role in the film and is helping with the marketing effort.

Thanks to the film's director Del Flores, who also designed and illustrated the book cover.

Every member of the cast and crew deserve the highest accolades:

Studio: K-T Films in association with Digital Ricky

Genre: Drama, Sports

Websites: comingsoon.net/films.php?id=84789 | facebook.com/pages/Live-For-Today/182364011823789

Director: Del Flores, and Kristin McKenzie

Screenwriter: Joe Barfield

Starring: Denver Danyla, Kristin McKenzie, Lexi Midmay, Miguel

Mora, and Brian Matthew Carr

Produced by: Lucia Barfield, Carla Earhart, Darrell Supercinski, Brian Carr, and Eric Foty.

Trailer editing by Ricardo Casco.

Thanks to my book editor, Melanie Saxton, for falling in love with the story and sharing it with others.

I'm not a marketing genius. I'm an engineer with a story to share. I thank the publications who have interviewed me. Gaining traction and spreading the word is a monumental task. Please share our Facebook page and help us publicize an important movie as we address themes of bullying, suicide and redemption.

MIRACLES

Do you believe in Miracles? Most scoff at miracles, but they cannot be denied. We always associate miracles with prayers but some feel their prayers go unanswered. Occasionally a tragedy precedes miracles. Many people are cured miraculously and there is no other way it can be described other than a miracle. There are stories of those who missed a flight only to learn the flight crashed and all aboard died. Some miracles leave a tragedy in its wake. A miracle for the person who missed the flight and survived? Maybe. But it was a tragedy for those who died. Even the Bible is clear on miracles; for instance David and Goliath. The Philistines were defeating Israel and King Saul. The mightiest of Saul's armies could not defeat the mighty Goliath. It was then a small boy told Saul he could defeat Goliath. They all laughed at David who was armed with only a slingshot and a rock. David killed Goliath. It was a miracle! From the Philistines point of view it was impossible and a tragedy for they lost to Saul's armies.

The story, Live For Today, would never have occurred if not for the miracle that happened to Joe Willis Renfro. It began during World War II. Joe was an engineer for the Navy and trained at the Naval Air Station in Corpus Christi, Texas. He was to coordinate construction on an island called Okinawa in the Pacific so American troops could invade Japan. Many feared it was a suicidal mission from which most would not return. His best friend Lance Russell trained as an alternate with Joe, who was to lead the mission. At the age of 22 he was the most qualified engineer. His wife Beverly or Bea as he called her stayed on base while their two year old daughter Sue stayed with Joe's parents in Saint Joseph, Missouri.

The two families lived on the base. Lance's wife, Mary, was pregnant and Lance had already decided the baby would be a boy. He intended to name his son after himself.

A few weeks before Joe was to be sent on his mission he managed to snatch a three day pass with his wife. He wrote and sent a thank you letter to his parents to bring their daughter Sue to meet them on their short getaway.

Dear Folks,

I got the package and thank you ever so much. Bee and I will have our christmas and be thinking of you. The only package I opened was the socket, and I really appreciated it. If you can I would appreciate some of my shorts, a couple of spoons and a knife. You just can't buy silverware down here.

I guess I'll be going to Kentucky before long and when I do maybe we can meet somewhere along the line. I don't know where Morehead is but maybe you can figure some place where we could see each other for a litte while. I would give anything if you could bring Sue.

I can't express my thoughts this Christmas with gifts but I hope this letter will convey my thoughts. I will be with you in spirit on christmas morning.

I wish you a very merry Christmas and a New year that will bring Victory and a Christmas that will see us all together again. May this be our last year of destruction on this earth and may the Lord see fit to bring "Peace on earth, and good will towards men".

I remain forever and ever,

Your loving son,

Joe Willis

(The actual letter Joe Willis wrote in 1945)

Unbeknownst to Joe, his wife prayed daily that her husband would not be killed in battle. Inside she knew Joe would never return. The prayers continued.

Upon his return from the three-day leave, Joe immediately did final training sessions. The day was overcast. This was when they discovered Joe was color blind and could not differentiate many of the battle flags. He was immediately pulled and not allowed to participate in the attack. His best friend, Lance, took his position.

Was it a miracle Joe was not sent into battle or did God answer Bea's prayers?

(The real Bea and Joe Willis 1942)

Lance was sent to battle in Joe's place at a small island called Okinawa only 340 miles from the mainland of Japan. The attack began on April 1, 1945 and lasted 82 days. One of the fiercest and deadly battles of the war in the Pacific, with American losses at 20,000 dead and 55,000 wounded. The

Japanese lost between 77,000 and 110,000 dead. Lance landed on April 3 and was killed only a few hours after he arrived. The same day Joe and Bea were celebrating Joe's Birthday.

Two weeks later Mary learned of Lance's death. She went into shock and was rushed to the emergency room where she and her son died. Joe and Bea were devastated. Joe swore if he had a son he would name him Lance.

President Truman announced to the American people he had found a solution to bring the war to an end. A miracle that would prevent America from being forced to attack Japan on their own soil thus saving an estimated three million American lives and as many as fifteen million Japanese lives.

Truman's miracle was called the Manhattan Project. Little Boy and Fat Man did not bring a miracle to Hiroshima or Nagasaki. Still it was called a miracle and the war ended on September 2, 1945.

A miracle had happened. Joe had survived the war. He and Bea along with Sue remained in Corpus Christi to begin their new lives. Their favorite weekend place was Padre Island and the sandy shores along the Gulf of Mexico. Whenever time permitted they went to the beach. Sue loved the beach and she would go to the edge of the water, take off her swimsuit and venture into the saltwater. Joe had Bea had a difficult time keeping her out of the water. They led an Idyllic life and in 1949 another miracle came to them in the form of a son, Lance. Two years later they learned Bea was pregnant again. Late in the pregnancy they learned the baby might not survive. Again the family prayed and none more than Bea. A month later the doctors declared a miracle. They had no other explanation. The baby was now progressing normally. In celebration they went to Padre Island and celebrated with friends, cooking hotdogs and roasting marshmallows. They drank beer and told war stories. Then the unthinkable happened. Sue had disappeared. Frantically all searched for her, yelling her name but they heard no response. Bea discovered Sue's swimsuit at the water's edge.

The search continued for weeks. They never found Sue.

Do miracles happen? They are undeniable, but sometimes, bad things happen to good people. Most miracles are instant and can never be explained, other than by an act of God. But not all miracles are instant. Some of those miracles are rather a journey.

Chapter 1

SUMMER OF '61

Remember the first time you fell in love? The object of your affection most likely consumed every waking moment, lived in your dreams, and had your heart racing. Chances are, you probably thought it would last forever.

In the summer of 1961, Lance Renfro had everything. He was in love, had a great family, and had already plotted out his future. Lance was twelve-years-old.

We make plans, and God changes them. Sometimes life doesn't work out the way we anticipate. This was especially true for Lance.

A two-tone red and white Ford Edsel convertible flew down the highway, Lance sat in the back with Timmy, his younger brother. Both had hair buzzed short. Their father, Joe, was a naval officer during World War II and demanded they wear their hair "high and tight." Lance's crewcut was a little longer in front, and he combed it straight up with butch wax. Their father drove, and their mother Beverly filled the passenger seat.

Next to football, this was Lance's favorite time of year. Every summer his parents took a weekend trip to Neal's Cabins, not far from Kerrville, located near Garner State Park. He loved swimming in the Frio River. People from all around the country came to Neal's Cabins. This West Texas resort offered a retreat where occupants could relax and enjoy the cool, refreshing water.

The narrow two-lane asphalt highway took the family down a hill, just a few feet from the river. Lance glimpsed to his right and could see kids already swimming. The Texas summer was hot; the Frio River cold. Kids splashed in the waters of the Concan resort and enjoyed a break from the sweltering summer weather. Lance couldn't immediately see his favorite spot, but he knew where to find the "swing."

The road rose sharply more than thirty feet, then leveled off. Lance's father pulled off the road and parked in front of the resort office.

The four Renfro's bailed out of the car and stretched their legs. Their father wore khaki pants and a summer shirt, while their mother wore a long dress with her hair tied in a ponytail. Lance and Timmy were already dressed in trunks and anxious to hit the river. But first, they had to follow their parents into the office, then unload the car.

The resort office also served as a miniature grocery store. While Joe checked the reservation, Beverly picked out a few groceries with her sons. Sad-faced, both boys stared at the candy and comic books. Beverly smiled, reached into her purse, pulled out two coins. She extended a hand to each of her boys.

"Here, get what you want."

The boys each snatched a shiny new quarter. Lance scanned the comics and shortly picked a ten-cent *Superman* comic book. However, he debated on the second and could not choose between a ten-cent *Batman* comic or an *Amazing Fantasy 15*, a twelve-cent Marvel. The latter was a story was about a dorky boy who was teased by jocks on the school football team, and later acquired super powers through a spider bite. This new hero was called Spiderman.

Lance chose Spiderman, and with the remaining three-cents was able to get two pieces of Double Bubble gum for a penny, and one two-cent Hershey Bar. His quarter was gone, but he was fascinated with the Spiderman comic book. In many ways the boy, Peter Parker, was much like him—picked on, and always in trouble at home. Lance was always late, and always seemed to be doing something that didn't please his father… like failing to protect his brother. Lance identified with Peter, this mystery boy who became a super hero. Happy with his items, he returned to his mother.

The boys had their new treasures. Beverly had collected hot dogs, buns, and a can of chili, along with essential items they required for the weekend. Joe smiled at Beverly and shook the keys to the cabin over his head. Outside the office, he unrolled a pack of Camels from his shirtsleeve and lit up. Beverly did the same, but with a Salem Menthol.

All four hopped back into the Edsel. The engine rumbled to life, and they rolled slowly along a narrow crushed stone road to their cabin nestled on a bluff above the river. The area was dry, arid, and filled with diminutive oak trees, cedar trees, and prickly pear cactus. The pungent odor of the cedar filled the air. They pulled to a stop next to their cabin, took what they could carry from the car, and walked toward their getaway. Nearby, a roadrunner dashed across the landscape and disappeared into the brush.

Inside the rustic cedar and pine cabin, screens covered the windows. Beverly unloaded the food while the boys put away their clothes. Joe put his things in one of the bedrooms, , then suddenly another attack of his coughing spasms as he covered his mouth with a handkerchief.

"Sure wish I could get rid of this bronchitis."

Beverly said, "Hey Sugar, why don't you relax in the rocker outside, and I'll bring you a beer."

With a smile, Joe replied, "Thanks, Honey." He walked outside and endured another coughing spasm. He adjusted the old wooden rocking chair, settled into the cushion, and lit up another cigarette.

Beverly turned to the boys with a bright smile, and waved her hands for them to leave.

"Go. Enjoy the river before it gets too dark."

Lance and Timmy burst from the cabin only to have their father stop them. "Whoa."

Both boys skidded to a halt.

Joe grabbed Lance's shoulders. "Tiger, I want you to look after Timmy. Okay?"

"Yes, sir," said Lance.

Tiger was a nickname his father had bestowed when Lance was still in his playpen. The little boy would shake the bars and growl, causing Joe to laugh and comment, "Look at that little tiger." The name stuck. Everyone in the family called him "Tiger."

Joe grinned. "Enjoy the river."

Without a response, the boys tore from the cabin and raced for the river, leaving behind only a tiny dust cloud. Near the edge of the cliff a stair carved from the stone led down to the river a little more than thirty feet below. Tall cypress trees lined the banks and rose high above the cliff. All were more than five feet in diameter and all were perpetually watered from the flowing river, which widened and formed pools twenty feet or more in depth. The water so clear, it was easy to see the bottom.

Lance and Timmy reached the end of the stone stairs and continued to a boulder-filled spot on the bank. A few of the boulders were as enormous as a school bus and pierced the river at angles that had the bravest climbers scampering upward. One daring boy climbed to the top of a boulder and dove into the river below.

Half a dozen children and teenagers frolicked in the flowing water, enjoying the spring-fed, crystal clear blue waters that flowed swiftly through and around the limestone boulders.

Lance and Timmy passed these and other spots until they reached "the swing." They ran along a narrow trail skirting the river's edge until they came to a special opening. There the river was more than a hundred feet wide, and the cypress trees were abundant and tall. From one giant cypress hung a rope more than an inch in diameter. On the bank was an old stone and mortar set of stairs that ascended about five feet. Teenagers waited in line for the rope, with a few younger kids in tow.

At the top of the stairs, one gallant teenager held the rope suspended from the cypress. He gathered his courage, took a deep breath, and swung to the center of the river. He let go and plunged feet first. The rope swung back to the bank, and someone grabbed it and pulled it back to the stairs for the next person in line. The scenario played out over and over again as kids readied for their chance to jump.

Lance and Timmy got in line at the bottom of the stone stairs.

Two teenage girls laid on towels stretched out on the bank. Next to them, rock and roll blasted from a battery operated transistor radio. Summertime romance was in the air.

Finally, Lance was next in line. From the radio Elvis Presley sang, *Can't Help Falling in Love*. He heard the song, smiled and commented, "I like Elvis."

From behind him came a sweet, soothing voice. "Me too."

Lance turned and beheld the most beautiful girl he had ever seen in his life. Like an angel, her long wavy blond hair hung below her shoulders. He was dumbstruck.

She smiled sweetly. "What's your name?"

"Tiger," blurted Timmy.

"Tiger," Angel repeated.

Lance frowned and glared at his brother. Still, until the moment he heard the word "Tiger" roll from her mouth, his nickname had never sounded so cool.

She said, "I like it."

And for the first time in his life, so did Lance.

He pushed the rope toward Angel. "Here."

Surprised, Angel took the rope and prepared to swing.

"What's your name?" Lance asked.

She giggled. "Angel."

On the bank a girl screamed, "Go Angel!"

Angel smiled at Lance, turned away, grabbed the rope tight, swung out towards the water and plunged feet first into the cool Frio River.

Mesmerized, all Lance could do was watch as Angel swam to the bank. "Angel," he mumbled, oblivious to the rope handed to him.

A teenager stepped in front of Lance and grabbed the rope. "My turn," he yelled, "Flip."

Everyone turned to observe the teenager swing to the center of the river, where he executed a perfect flip. Most cheered, even Angel.

Again the rope was ready for Lance, but this time Timmy held it.

"C'mon Tiger, swing!"

"Okay, okay, Timmy." He took the rope and yelled, "Flip."

All within hearing distance turned to watch the brash kid do a flip. Most thought he was too young. Some laughed, a few resumed what they were doing, but many pinned their eyes on the spectacle to see how bad the results might be. They anticipated a proverbial wreck and gawked as Lance swung to the middle of the river and attempted the mid-air maneuver.

Well, the flip wasn't pretty, but Lance managed to penetrate the surface. Some of the teenagers actually applauded. So did Angel.

Lance swam to shore and pulled himself out next to the pretty girl whose blonde mane had recently captivated his attention and caused him to show off. He had barely settled in next to her when Timmy swung clumsily into the river. Lance kept a close eye on Timmy, just as he promised his father. Timmy choked and coughed as he surfaced. His movements were awkward as he splashed toward Lance. But he was able to crawl out of the river, and plopped down next to Angel's girlfriend.

Lance was nervous, yet excited. He had never felt this way in his life—a strange giddy feeling had his heart pounding from within his chest. As much as he tried to talk to Angel, everything coming out of his mouth sounded stupid. To him, everything Angel said was wonderful.

From the bluff a woman yelled, "Angel!"

Angel turned her head and waved to her mother.

"Time to come in."

"Okay, Mom," said Angel. She stood up as Lance scrambled to his feet.

"Gotta go."

Lance shrugged, "Sure. I'll walk you back."

Angel appeared pleased. Her girlfriend and Timmy trailed behind. For Lance, the world suddenly condensed into a new-found glory—Angel. When their shoulders touched or his hand brushed up against hers, the contact sent a thrill through his body.

Once upon the bluff, Angel turned to Lance. "Will I see you tomorrow, Tiger?"

His heart filled his throat, but he managed, "Sure, Angel."

His gaze followed her until she disappeared from sight. Still, he waited diligently in case she returned.

"Angel," he mumbled.

When Lance and Timmy reached their cabin, Timmy teased his brother.

"Lance has a girlfriend."

Even though he hated his brother's teasing, this time it didn't seem to matter. Waving his arms with excitement, he tried to describe Angel, the beautiful girl from the river, to mother and father. They thought Lance was cute as he fumbled with his words. He was determined to spend Saturday in Angel's company, and that night he thought about Angel as he read *Amazing Fantasy 15*. The story of Spiderman, the new comic book hero, paralleled his own life in so many ways. The only difference was that Peter Parker had super powers. Spiderman helped the weak, similar to the way Lance helped his brother Timmy. The only sad part was Spiderman's mistake that caused the death of his beloved Uncle Ben. Spiderman always blamed himself, and it was something he never forgot.

The next morning Lance shoved his breakfast down like an animal and ran to the river. He waited all morning, but never saw Angel. He had lunch with his parents and brother, but couldn't wait to return to the river. Again, his father told him to watch and protect Timmy. Angel didn't arrive until mid-afternoon, finally strolling up with her girlfriend.

On the Frio

All four swam in the river and floated around in huge black inner tubes. Slowly, Angel and Lance pulled away from her girlfriend and his brother. The two talked about all kinds of things. She was from Houston, and Lance shared that he was from Corpus Christi. For two young children like themselves, their home towns seemed to be a world apart. But that was a detail they could fix later. What they had was today.

Eventually, they came back to the swing where they first met. While Angel waited on the bank of the river, Lance swung from the rope again and quickly swam to shore. Their glorious time together passed all too quickly, ending when Angel's mother called again. She waved to her mother then turned to Lance, waiting for him to escort her.

He quickly checked the river and saw Timmy still floundering around. He grunted and thought, *Why not?* But he had promised his father.

With a groan Lance said, "You go. I gotta stay. My brother is still in the river."

Angel smiled. "Okay."

He watched as Angel and her friend walked away, and at that moment Lance hated his brother. He glared at Timmy, who was splashing toward him.

Angel stopped and turned back to ask Lance. "Are you going to the dance tonight?"

This was perfect! "Nothing can keep me away," he promised.

His eyes continued to track Angel as she climbed the stone stairs that led to the top of the bluff. Just before she disappeared from sight, she turned and looked back at him. As she grinned and waved. Lance almost choked on his heart as she disappeared from sight.

In the meantime, somehow Timmy managed to pull himself from the river

"I'm going to ask Angel to go steady at the dance," Lance announced to his soggy little brother.

Timmy giggled. "Tiger is in love."

Even Lance laughed as his mind filled with wondrous thoughts about Angel. Soon she would be his girlfriend! This was the happiest day of his life. He continued to stare at the spot on the ridge where Angel had vanished, hoping she might return one more time. He was in another world and happy beyond belief.

Perhaps this distraction contributed to what happened next. As coordinated and athletic as Lance was, he slipped on a wet muddy stone. His feet flew out from beneath him, high up in the air, and he landed on his head. That was the last thing he remembered.

***

Lance laid motionless in the hospital bed, surrounded by his family. A doctor bent over the bed with a stethoscope, while his mother stood on the other side, anxiously awaiting the doctor's response. She held Lance's hand. Joe stood next to his wife. At the foot of the bed Timmy stood on a stool and peered at his brother.

Lance moaned.

"He's coming around," said the doctor.

Beverly rubbed his hand, "Lance? Lance?"

Slowly, Lance moved and rolled his head. A smile filled his face.

"Angel," he mumbled as his eyes fluttered and opened. Quickly, his smile disappeared. Bewildered and confused, he shot erect in the hospital bed and tried to scramble to his feet.

The doctor grabbed him, "Whoa! Hold on there, young man."

Still confused, Lance looked to his parents for help. "Mom, Dad, you don't understand! Angel is at the dance."

"That was last night, Lance," said Beverly.

"No! I'm going to ask her to go steady."

Relieved, they all laughed.

Timmy said, "Tiger is in love. My brother has a girlfriend."

Frustrated, Lance snapped at his brother, "Quit calling me Tiger."

Joe and Beverly laughed again, happy that their son's brain was functioning.

Joe Renfro tried to console his son. "We'll be back next year, son."

Dismayed, Lance said, "But it will be too late."

"Don't worry, Sugar. You'll see her next summer," consoled Beverly.

Joe continued to chuckle, but it abruptly turned into a cough, then a violent hack. For a moment all eyes turned away from the patient as Joe gasped for breath.

The doctor's eyebrows furrowed with real concern. "You need to have that cough checked," he announced.

Joe waved his hands in the air. "It's nothing, Doc."

***

The return home was uneventful, other than Beverly pushing Joe to go to the doctor. Beverly, an expert at maneuvering her husband and boys into any number of motherly requests, felt relieved. Joe still believed he had bronchitis brought on by allergies, but her charm worked, and he would now get a medical opinion. Fortunately for them all, Beverly was the kind of woman all children wanted as a mother and any man would want for a wife. It was impossible to say no to her.

But more weighty issues concerned Lance. *What about Angel? Was she gone forever?*

He continued to fret, then asked his mother, "How will I find Angel? What will I do?"

Beverly smiled at Lance. She was a fan of James Stewart, and after seeing the movie *The Man Who Knew too Much* she frequently hummed Doris Day's iconic song. And so she answered Lance with a tune:

Que sera, sera.
Whatever will be, will be.
The future's not ours to see.
Que sera, sera.
What will be, will be.

"Aw, Mom," said Lance. He didn't want a song. More essential things were on his mind than his father's allergies or his mother's ancient lyrics. He had just lost his first love. He wanted to find Angel.

His mother smiled at him and continued to hum.

How would he let Angel know about his head injury? More than anything in the world, he wanted to be at that dance. Yet he didn't show up, and Angel deserved an explanation.

Reality set in. *Contact her.* That became his overriding mission, although there were obstacles. The only thing he remembered was her name: Angel. He didn't even know her last name or the number of her cabin. He couldn't recall the name of Angel's friend. Lance asked his brother and prayed Timmy might remember, but Timmy didn't even remember Angel's first name.

Lance scribbled down everything that came to mind, which wasn't much, and tucked the notes in his new Amazing Fantasy 15 comic book. Soon he realized he might never see her again unless she returned the next summer. There was no picture, no trinket, nothing they had traded or given each other. All he would ever have of Angel were his memories of their time together, and of course, the swing where it all began.

***

Beverly believed it was essential to have moral faith in a Supreme Being. In her opinion, Christians were good, upstanding people. For this reason, she not only made sure the family prayed before every meal, but she kept the boys active in church. Although the Renfro's took a hiatus when they vacationed at Neal's Cabins, that was the exception rather than the rule.

Lance and Timmy always went to Sunday school before the sermon. Their mother taught one of the adult classes, and Joe would sometimes attend. But most of the time he was busy working on cars to make extra cash. It fell on his shoulders to pay the bills and scrape a few dollars into savings.

Regardless, Beverly made sure Timmy and Lance were dressed in their finest little suits and attended the First Methodist Church of Corpus Christi each and every Sunday. She checked and straightened their ties and made sure her sons dressed properly.

At bedtime, she listened intently while her boys said their prayers. Lance and Timmy knelt at the side of the bunk bed, bowed their heads, clasped their hands together, and spoke the same prayer while their mother stood over them and listened. Lance had memorized the words:

Now I lay me down to sleep.
I pray the Lord my soul to keep.
If I should die before I wake,
I pray the Lord my soul to take.

Lance was also at church for Tuesday night Boy Scout meetings for Troop 175. All of his friends were Boy Scouts; Jay Defee, Steve Boyd, Lloyd Cage, Todd Samuels, Chuck Russell, and Hal Bass. They did everything together, from fishing to football. This was the best group of friends a guy could have. Beverly had also been the den mother for Cub Scouts and all the boys loved her.

Their minister, Barcus Moore, gave the Sunday morning sermons. For the boys, the sermons were boring and the long wooden pews dreadfully uncomfortable. Lance had the hardest time staying awake, and he always believed that was why his mother made him and his brother wear ties. When they dozed off, she'd jerk on their ties real quick. Instantly they'd be wide awake, at least for a few minutes.

When Lance managed to stay awake, he did listen intently and remembered some of the topics on which Barcus Moore preached.

"God answers all prayers, if you have faith!" Barcus made an emphasis on the word "faith." After a long pause he continued, "God will answer your prayer. With faith, anything is possible."

Lance got wide-eyed and excited. This would solve his dilemma! He said a silent prayer during the service, and that night in his bunk bed repeated it: "God, please help me find Angel." Reassured and excited, he went to sleep. He continued to say the same prayer every night.

A few months later, Joe's lingering cough became worse. He became sick and ultimately had to stay home from work for a few days—which was extremely unusual, for he never missed a day on the job. When he returned to work, he didn't appear to get any better.

Finally Joe was admitted to the hospital. After he was discharged, he stayed at home with orders to relax and stay away from the office. For a few weeks he actually went to church with his wife and boys. Lance never fell asleep when his father was in church.

One Sunday morning, Lance heard the minister talk about healing the sick. He even saw Barcus Moore heal an elderly woman by holding his hand over her head and announcing that if she had faith, God would take away her pain. She turned around and shouted with joy that she no longer felt any pain. It was a miracle, and Lance never forgot the sight. He adored and trusted his minister.

Meanwhile, Joe continued to get worse and seemed to always be tired. He stayed in bed or watched television, mostly *Perry Mason* and *Gunsmoke*.

The more Lance watched his father, the more concerned he became. He remembered the woman Barcus Moore had healed, and so at night prayed for God to cure his father. This was in addition to his special prayer for Angel. He had no doubt God would answer his prayers.

Joe's parents had come from Missouri to help. Lance knew his father was sick but his Grandmother, Audrey, acted like she was the one who was sick and dying. Audrey would lay on the couch with a wet rag over her head while crying, "How can this be happing to me!"

Although Lance didn't understand he could feel the tension. He understood his father was sick and it was serious.

A few days later Lance's mother told him he had been invited to spend a few days with his best friend, Bobby Harris. He was excited when Bobby's mother, Betty, picked him up and drove him to their house in her new Buick.

Before Lance could scramble from the car, Betty stopped him and said, "Wait Lance, I need to tell you something."

Lance smiled and sat back in his seat.

"Lance, your father is going to die."

Lance was dazed. The shock of her words paralyzed him.

Betty said nothing more other than those few fatal words no young boy wants to ever hear. He initially refused to believe her. *This is impossible.*

She went into the house, while Lance stayed in the car. His mind became a boiling cauldron of fear and panic.

"Not my father!" Lance cried out. Scared, and hurt at the bombshell, Lance had so many questions. Nevertheless, he also had faith that God would help his father. He took comfort in Minister Moore's words: "God answers all prayers."

That night, he recited the bedtime prayer his mother had taught him, then smiled and added, "God, please make my father well." He finished with, "And help me find Angel." Lance was convinced his prayers would prove Betty wrong. God would fix things. She would see.

***

While Lance stayed at his friend's house things got worse with his grandparents and his parents. Joe's parents had become a liability and no longer an asset. He knew he was dying and what time remained he wanted to spend with his sons and not listening to his mother whine. He wanted to be with his wife and he knew only days remained before he would be unable to know what was happening. He wanted a little peace whatever that might be. Joe ordered his parents to leave and a few days after they returned home he managed to type a letter to his parents expressing his feelings:

Saturday night

Dear Folks,

I may never send this letter, just burn it instead, but there are some things that I feel it is time to say. I enjoyed the cheerful tone in Dads voice and certainly appreciated the fact that he at no time mentioned my illness, but instead talked of cheerful things. Mother, appraently the letter I wrote did you absoutely no good whatsoever, as I could not help but notice the quiver in your voice and the constant effort on your part to have me say something to cheer you up. Also as to the letters, I don't see where Bea is doing so badly, for I noticed you have not had time to answer my last letter, but in the same space of time I have received two from Dad. Now here it is, for I am damn tired of witholding any bad news from you. The Doctor told me that I am not and cannot be cured. It can reoccur at any time and also he has said there is a possibility I might live 30 more years. However, it did reoccur. Two weeks ago a large lump came on my neck and it was diagnosed as malignant. X-Ray treatments were started immediately and so far it has responded and decreased in size. You realize that X-Ray can't be used in all places. I have lost weight down to 151 pounds and it is a great strain to even walk through the house. Bea is driving me to the doctors as it takes all I have to drive the car. The pain is so severe that an open prescription has been left at the drugstore for codine. I can go no more than two hours, day or night without it. When I sleep as much as an hour and a half I feel I have really done something. I have uncontrollable diarrhea. Yes, I even go in the bed. I spent three and a half hours in front of the commode the last week with the heaves. You asked how I felt and there it is. Had you written one cheerful letter I would never have told you. Bea was forbidden to do so. The last thing in this world I want is sympathy. We do not even talk about me around the house. I told you I have no time for unpleasant thoughts and I meant it. Don't go running down here as I don't want you. Until you can come through the door with a smile and stay out of the bedroom where you cried when you were here before, I would rather you would stay in St. Joe. Don't start any conversation about me being your child and that making things different, for if you were really concerned about me I think you would try to introduce a little cheer in stead of the constant gloom.

I could sit around the house all day and cry about the wife and children I may very possibly leave but wouldn't that do a lot of good. I love this house and everyone in it, so I am going to do nothing to make it unpleasant for anyone. I instead have high hopes of going back to work and living a normal life. As long as humanly possible that is the way it will work. I want nothing, absolutely NOTHING to interfere with the happiness we have in this house. I don't want you to even mention anything about this again. It seems rather stupid that I should have called tonight just for your benefit. It is high time you stopped feeling sorry for yourself, as I don't know of any reasons you have for it. You continually get on the subject that I am your child, well here is another kick for you- About four years ago one of my children had an illness diagnosed as epilepsy. It has gotten a great deal better and we constantly hope for complete recovery. I am not even going to tell you which one. The only person I feel sorry for in the whole deal is Bea. If I go under she has three children to raise, one with a dread disease, and only a pittance of insurance to do it on. You mention the things you have worked so hard for, well, what about our house and everything in it? We have both worked very hard and of course Bea could not keep it. How do you think she feels when she helps me on with my clothes, and helps me wash even? She may end up supporting a cripple for many years, but in all this ordeal she has been nothing but kind and helpful. She gets up at night with me and rubs my back to help me go back to sleep and I am very greatful to say that never once has she had anything but a smile on her face. Why can't you spread a little cheer in this world? Lord nows it needs it.

I sincerly hope you can change your outlook on life and quit thinking what a bad deal you have had. I hate to write such a letter as this, but you have been rubbibg me raw ever since you were here. I hope you will see fit to us having a little cheer and happiness together. Just don't ever start off a conversation with me by telling me how tough things are for I don't think you know what real trouble is.

Try to find a cheerful thought and put it on paper.

Love and kisses,

Bea gave him all the love she could in her husband's final days. She convinced him not to send the letter.

***

A week passed, and Lance was still at his friend's house. The more he prayed, the better he felt. Every night he continued his prayer ritual, and one morning when Betty told him during breakfast that he didn't have to go to school.

"Your mother's coming to get you," she said.

Lance was excited. God had answered his prayers! He just knew his father was okay and his mother was coming to take him home. He couldn't wait until his mother arrived and missed her happy, smiling face.

When he heard the front door open, Lance ran to greet her, but he stopped abruptly. Something was terribly wrong. His mother's smile had vanished; her eyes were red and wet. She went to her knees and pulled Lance to her, then made a soft moaning sound as she whispered in his ear, "Daddy's gone."

Pins pricked his body and Lance suddenly felt sick to his stomach. Confusion flooded his mind.

"No, no, Daddy's not gone!"

It couldn't be true, because he had prayed to God to make it better. Didn't God answer all prayers?

***

No one is ever prepared for death, least of all the Renfro family. People filled the church for the funeral. Dressed in black, Beverly walked to the casket and reached in to touch the face of her husband. She stepped back and let Lance and Timmy see their father one last time. The boys stood motionless. They didn't really understand death.

"Daddy is asleep, Mommy," said Timmy.

Beverly tried to hold back her tears. Lance frowned at Timmy as he studied his father and wondered why all of this was happening. He thought his father looked a lot better than he had the last few months when he was sick.

Through her tears Beverly managed, "Yes Timmy, Daddy is asleep."

She and Timmy walked away.

Lance hesitated, then bent near his father, and whispered, "Daddy, wake up." He shook his father's shoulder. "Wake up, Daddy." Then Lance touched his father's face and gained a true understanding of death. He jerked his hand away from his father's stone cold, lifeless body.

Questions raced through Lance's mind as tears rolled down his cheeks. Why had God ignored him? What had he done wrong? He must be a bad sinner if God didn't have time for his prayers.

His minister's words haunted him: "With faith, anything is possible." Again, he gazed at his father. Lance understood only two things. First, God had not answered his prayers. Secondly, God would have kept his father alive if only Lance had enough faith.

Later, he heard people offer many reasons: "God needed Joe in Heaven," or, "He must have been a sinner," or, "It was God's will."

Lance also heard a woman say, "He must not have had enough faith."

What faith Lance had developed in his young life wavered. God had abandoned him.

***

Life would never be the same. It was as if the family's joy withered and died along with Joe. Beverly took her boys to church a few more times.

One Sunday morning Lance woke up, saw the time, and realized they were almost late for church. He rushed to the door of his mother's room and peeked in. She was still in bed. He decided to be ready by the time she woke. He dressed Timmy and himself and double-checked their ties. Finally, he went to his mother's bedroom and shook her.

"Mom, it's time to get up. We're late for church."

She rolled over and smiled at Lance. Dried tears covered her cheeks and her eyes were red. "We'll go next week, Lance."

Then she rolled back and drew the covers over her head.

He just stood there, then silently backed out of her room. Timmy was hungry, so Lance headed to the kitchen and made breakfast just like his mother always had. He cut a grapefruit in half, careful to slide the knife down each juicy section. Finally, he cut around the back so each piece would come out with a spoon. A sprinkle of brown sugar topped the slices. Next came two pieces of toast with a lot of butter, sugar and cinnamon powder. He even started a pot of coffee for his mother.

She slept all day.

The next Sunday brought more of the same, except this time Lance couldn't rouse his mother. She moaned, but did not wake up. He carefully removed the Jim Beam bottle out of her right hand and pulled away the remains of a cigarette from between her fingers.

They never went to church again. Soon, she quit praying at dinner.

Only the nightly prayer remained. His mother still walked in and made sure he and Timmy prayed before they went to sleep. One night, Lance climbed down from the top bunk bed and assumed his position with his brother Timmy. When he looked up at his mother, her sad face was wet with tears. As was more and more her habit, one hand was a half full bottle of bourbon and in the other a burning cigarette.

"Night, boys..." Beverly turned and walked to her bedroom.

Lance made Timmy say the prayer with him. The same thing happened the next night. His mother never came into their room to say the bedtime prayer again. Eventually his brother refused.

One night as he laid in the top bunk, Lance clasped his hands in front of his chest and prepared to say a prayer. Timmy was already asleep.

He closed his eyes tight. "Now I lay me down... "

He stopped. With eyes wide open, he stared at the white stucco ceiling. "Why?" he asked God and burst into tears.

Lance cried hard. He rolled over, buried his face in his pillow, and continued to cry, as though his heart were breaking for the hundredth time.

He never said another prayer. His wavering faith was now lost.

***

Lance and Timmy sat at the table and ate quietly. Before each was peeled-back aluminum TV dinner. This time they ate enchiladas. Their mother had barely managed to heat up the food.

No longer was she the beautiful, pin-up brunette she had once been. Though still attractive, she was a bit haggard around the edges and appeared older than her thirty-two years. In one hand she held a glass of bourbon—no ice, no water. Between two fingers on her other hand dangled what seemed to be a perpetually burning cigarette. She snuffed it out in an oddly-shaped green glass ashtray filled to the brim with ashes and butts.

As she lit another cigarette, Beverly observed the boys closely, waiting for the right moment. She wanted to tell them, but it was difficult. Finally she blurted, "Boys, we're moving to California."

Both boys were upset. Timmy was almost in tears and stubbornly shook his head.

Lance was confused. "What?"

"We're moving to California," she said with a sigh.

Timmy jumped up and screamed, "No!" He ran to his bedroom.

"Timmy!" she yelled after him.

Lance stood and waited until his mother turned back to him.

"I don't want to go."

"I have a job, Lance. I have no other choice. We'll be with your Aunt." She started to cry. "Lance, please help me."

When he nodded, she knew she had his attention. "You know your brother is special." She grabbed Lance's shoulders. "You must be the man of the house and help me raise Timmy. You need to protect him. He's your little brother. Please?"

Doing his best to be a man, Lance braced himself and squared his shoulders. "Okay, Mom."

"Promise?"

"I promise."

Relieved, she released her physical hold on Lance. "Good. And Lance, remember, Timmy doesn't have a father anymore." Sad eyes tried to smile at him, but tears soon welled up and spilled over. Slowly, she turned and walked away. Even though she was gone from the room, she retained her mental hold and dominance over Lance—a hold that was unbreakable.

"I promise, Mom," he mumbled, again.

Lance's dreams and future ended with that promise. He was given the burden of a man, yet he was still a child.

Chapter 2

THE CLASS OF '67

Rock and Roll was in full swing during the summer of 1967. The Beatles, Doors, and Rolling Stones ruled the airwaves. However, on the California shore the Beach Boys were king and surfing was the thing.

Cars lined the Malibu beach. An old yellow "woodie," trimmed with wood and surfing racks blared music from the speakers through the open doors. Jan and Dean's, *Ride the Wild Surf*, rolled across the sandy beach. No song could have been more appropriate. Monstrous waves pounded the shore. Only the brave and foolish challenged those monsters. Surfers wore "baggies" and a wetsuit top to protect against the frigid Pacific Ocean. Young surf specialists continued to charge the giant surf, only to be tossed about and thrown back to the beautiful white sand.

A perfect wave rolled in and six surfers managed to catch the giant. One dropped away, while another disappeared into the wave. Four brave hearts managed to secure a ride. Slowly, the wave formed a perfect pipeline; only two boys entered. One was sucked into the wave. A blond and bronzed stalwart soul remained in the wave, determined to finish what would be a perfect ride.

Surfers and spectators alike gawked and pointed to the lone gallant surfer. A cheer rose when he managed to finish the ride, still on his board. Lance Renfro had just mastered what few could and was all grins as he sloshed ashore. Surfers came to congratulate him, while others stared in awe at the local surfing hero.

Lance walked toward the woodie where he laid down his board. He shook his hair and ran his hands through his long blond locks. The old butch hairstyle was gone, exchanged out for a longer style that almost covered his ears.

Nearby, two surfers waxed their boards. One of the surfers shook his head and said to Lance, "Awesome ride, Lance."

"Thanks."

"I don't think I would've ridden that cruncher. Hey, Lance, can you make me another stick?"

"Sure, get with me later. Longboard or big gun?"

"BIG waves."

"You need a big gun."

The other surfer said, "You going out for track this year?"

Lance snickered and with a wave of his arm toward the surf he said, "With all this? No way."

***

The East L.A. High School was average-sized. Students mulled around the building waiting for the bell. The students segregated themselves into groups: athletes, surfers, and others. A gold Honda 350 rolled into the parking area and stopped near the surfers. Lance dismounted and locked his Honda just as the bell rang. Although new, he had slightly modified his motorcycle with the Malibu touch. The handlebars were reversed so he had to lean forward more and not sit erect. His Honda had more of a racing style instead of the stock appearance. He had also added special "tittie" grips on the handlebars and custom air filters to the carburetors just below the gas tank. A custom exhaust had replaced the stock pipes. All the modifications cost him nothing. Everything had been done in exchange for one of his custom-made surfboards. Without a care in the world, he strolled casually to his first class.

Two hours later, Lance was dressed and on the field for his physical education class.

Coach Clements observed Lance intently as he made the students run around the track. In the middle of the pack, Lance loafed along with his friends. When the bell rang, all the students headed for the gym but Coach Clements pulled Lance to the side.

"Lance, you excel at team sports. If you play, you can win a scholarship."

Instantly, the carefree surfer disappeared. Lance became angry and his answer had an intense hostility. "I don't do team sports, Coach."

"School's almost out for the summer, Renfro. We need you on the team next year."

"Sorry, Coach. I have other priorities."

"Son, don't throw away your God-given talent."

Lance grunted, "Is that all, Coach?"

Coach Clements sighed and waved Lance away. *What a waste of talent*, he thought, wondering why an athlete like Lance would throw away an opportunity.

***

The smell of fiberglass resin permeated the garage. Lance worked diligently on two surfboards. The epoxy began to harden on the yellow surfboard as he shaved and formed the foam on another board. His work was a thing of beauty.

The door to the kitchen creaked open and Beverly poked her head out. A smile lit her face. "Dinner's ready."

"Not hungry, Mom."

She shook her head. "Are you sure? I have green beans, potatoes, and ham."

Lance stopped his work and turned to his mother. He grinned, "My favorite?"

"Yes."

"Cornbread?"

"Of course, and plenty of butter."

Lance laid his tools aside. "Give me a minute to clean up."

A few minutes later, Lance gorged himself on his favorite meal. Beverly puffed on a cigarette as she washed dishes, looking frail and weak. She scrutinized Lance closely. Something was on her mind, and she appeared anxious. She waited for Lance to finish, and when he pushed the plate away she walked to the table, sat across from her son, and announced, "We're moving back to Texas."

Lance was stunned and upset. "No. I want to finish school here!"

"I'm sorry, Lance."

"All my friends are here. I don't want to go back to Corpus Christi."

"We're moving to Houston."

"What?" Lance was stunned. "If you're gonna move back to Texas, at least go home. Go back to Corpus."

"Too many bad memories."

"Why Houston?"

"Bob is there."

The words astonished Lance. "Dad's best friend?"

She nodded and tried to smile. "He wants to marry me."

Stunned, he peered across the table at his mother and shook his head. "Mom…"

"Lance, I don't want to go into it now, but there are too many things that have happened. You know what I'm talking about. I must leave here."

On the verge of desperation, Lance pleaded one more time, "Mom."

"Please, Lance," Beverly, begged. "There are other things you don't understand. Besides it would be good for us to get away from here. You know what I mean? We need a fresh start."

His shoulders sagged in defeat, something he was not familiar with. "When?"

With the worst over, Beverly relaxed. "In a week."

"A week? But it's summer and this will be my senior year."

"Please, Lance."

"Mom… " The news brought Lance's world down. He already had enough problems, and this was too much. His life was crumbling all over again.

"Promise me you'll go." She hesitated, and for the first time she could remember Lance failed to promise. His lack of response alarmed her. "I need you."

Lance continued to stare at his mother.

She tried to change the direction of the conversation and lighten up the atmosphere, "Hey, maybe you'll find that dream girl again. Remember? Angel, wasn't it? Didn't she live in Houston?"

Lance remembered and a thin smile crossed his lips... but only for a moment. "Dreams don't come true." Lance grabbed a piece of cornbread and said, "I gotta go."

When he reached his Honda he kick started it and took off.

Lance cruised along the California coast down Highway 101. Flying past cars, his mother's awful news caused him to be borderline reckless.

He cruised down the beach and stopped near the sand dune. He got off the motorcycle and sat in the sand, where he pulled out his pocket knife and glared at the thing as if it was his real problem. Tears rolled from his eyes as hee carved a beautiful number "43" in the sand. Something tormented him tremendously. He turned his palm up and put the blade on his wrist. He started to bring the sharp blade across his wrist but stopped. He closed the knife, sighed and stared out to the lonely waves.

The threat of the move ruined everything. His friends, his life—they were all in California. There was nothing for him in Texas. Especially in Houston.

***

The sign over the door read: ARMY RECRUITING OFFICE. Lance checked the sign before entering the office. A few minutes later, Lance was seated in front of a Recruiting Officer who peered at Lance's identification. A poster of the adventure in Vietnam adorned one wall.

The officer shook his head and handed the ID back to Lance. "Sorry, son. We require you be eighteen to join. Get a parent's release or come back when you turn eighteen."

Devastated at the information Lance stood up, put away his license and walked out.

***

Stars lit up the sky as traffic rushed past the serene beach. Lance leaned against his motorcycle and sipped from a long neck beer. Music floated over the beach as the exterior lights from a nearby club barely lit up the beach. He sat there and stared into the tranquil surf. In one hand he held a pocketknife. He kept rolling it in his hand. Sometimes he'd flip it in the air and catch it without looking, as though he'd done it a thousand times.

"How could she?" Lance mumbled.

He didn't want to go. Strangely, he didn't want to stay, either. Lance didn't care anymore. There had to be another way. He stared at the knife in his hand. He opened it and flipped some more, catching it perfectly each time. Two girls in bikinis walking along the water's edge talked excitedly about something of importance as they neared him.

How could she marry Bob? Why move? He just couldn't believe it. He knew his mother had to go on with her life, but as far as he was concerned his life was now over.

As the couple walked past, Lance caught a bit of the conversation

One of the girls said, "That's right Elvis Presley married Priscilla yesterday."

"You're kidding?"

"No."

Lance grunted. He could no longer hear the girls but what did it matter to him? Other things raced through his mind.

He took the handle of the knife in one hand and turned his other palm up. He placed the blade against his wrist. *Quick and easy, no more problems,* he thought.

Tears filled his eyes. He moved the knife away from his wrist, closed it, and put it back in his pocket.

He had to help his mother, even if he didn't want to go to Texas. He deliberated about Bob. Actually, he liked his father's best friend. It might even be good for his mother. He sighed, stood up, and stared into the surf. In a fit of conflicted anger he screamed and threw the beer bottle into the ocean. From the nearby club drifted the song, *California Nights*.

"How appropriate," he muttered. Then suddenly, Lance was calm. Nothing really mattered. Barefoot he straddled his motorcycle, kicked out the stand, and started the engine. For a long time he stared at the beach. With one last look, he roared away in the night.

Chapter 3

HOUSTON AND NEW FRIENDS

The move to Houston went as well as could be expected. Lance had already unloaded his Honda. He continued to help Bob and his mother empty the van of their personal items and put things in the proper rooms. The duplex was located on the west side of Houston. Lance, Beverly, and Bob continued hauling boxes from moving van to the house. It took a considerable portion of the day to unload it all, but it would take weeks to organize their new home.

Bed frames, box springs and mattresses were the first order of business. Then the other furniture was moved into position. The kitchen was another priority, and Lance arranged the dishes, silverware and pans in their designated places.

Bob walked in. Instantly, Lance noticed he was concerned about something.

"Where's Mom?" Lance said.

"Sleeping."

"She did look tired."

"Listen Lance, we need to talk." Bob hesitated and wrung his hands together. "Your mother is sick."

"What do you mean?"

Bob fidgeted, unsure of what to say. Finally he blurted out, "Leukemia."

At the devastating word, Lance's world crumbled a little more. He couldn't believe his ears, but there was no mistaking what was clearly written on Bob's face.

"I'm doing everything I can, but we don't know if she's going to pull through."

Lance felt like someone had just punched him in the stomach. Part of him refused to believe it, but at the same time his mind said, *Not again!*

Lance's voice was shaky and unsure, "She'll be okay!"

Bob took a deep breath and let it out. Hesitant, he shook his head.

Lance put down the plates. "I've gotta go." He started to walk away.

Bob said, "Lance!"

Lance fled through the front door to the comfort of his motorcycle and roared off.

***

Fast and reckless, Lance raced down Houston's unfamiliar streets.

There was very little light for nighttime driving and all he had to guide him was the Honda's lone headlight. He roared west along Westheimer's narrow and dangerous two-lane asphalt road until he reached Hillcroft. A Sinclair station was on the left and next to it was a Jack-In-the-Box. On the southwest corner stood a new shopping center lined with a half-dozen new stores. The northwest corner was vacant with a property line skirted in barbed wire.

Concentrating straight ahead, Lance saw nothing but rice fields in the distance. He pulled into the Sinclair station and checked his billfold. All he had was two dollars. He used 78 cents to put two gallons in the tank. After he paid, he walked to the Jack-In-the-Box and ordered the Jack Burger with Jack's Secret Sauce for twenty-two cents, a large chocolate malt for a quarter, and two tacos for fifty cents. His meal came out to a grand total of ninety-seven cents.

When the meal was finished, he mounted his Honda and tried to decide where to go. He turned right and started north, driving away from the rice fields and heading… somewhere. Anywhere.

His tears left dusty trails down his cheeks. He crossed Buffalo Bayou and decided to turn around. He sped along a street called Woodway past some apartments and continued for a few miles until he reached the Tanglewood subdivision. The streets were lined with expensive houses. He wound through until he found Buffalo Bayou again.

Finally, he came to an area where there were no more houses. The land had reverted to its natural wild state and the woods and darkness were what he presently desired. His Honda meandered through a maze of trees down an extremely narrow dirt path through the brush that led to the bayou. When he reached the bayou's bank he parked and walked to the water's edge, plopping himself on the ground. Tears once again welled up in his eyes. He stood erect, pulled out his pocket knife and began to carve something on a tree. He worked furiously, carving the number "43." He closed the knife and put it in his pocket. He stared at the number, wrapped his arms around himself and rocked back and forth. He moaned and tears again rolled from his eyes.

Lance wanted oblivion.

He leaned over slightly and slid the knife from his pocket. He flipped it a few times, then stopped and held it up. His mind reflected on the history the knife hid. The blade shimmered in the moonlight about a foot in front of his face. He gazed at it intently, mesmerized by the cold steel.

He brought his other hand near his knife and turned his wrist up facing the heavens. For a long while he sat motionless and continued to stare at both hands. Suddenly he closed the knife and slipped it back in his pocket. As he wept, he pulled his feet near so he could wrap his hands around his knees.

Lance stayed in this position for a few minutes, then groaned and shook his head in a mixture of despair and anger, still wondering why it had all happened. He would not wait any longer and without a moment's hesitation pulled the knife back out of his pocket, flipped open the sharp blade, and exposed his wrists before him. Lance tilted the blade to a vertical position and pressed it into his flesh until it made a small puncture. The trickle of blood rolled down to the moist earth beneath him. The artery in his wrist pulsed with excitement. As tears flooded his vision, he saw Angel in his mind's eye and a slight smile came to his gritted lips. He could see Spiderman. Thoughts flashed through his mind at the speed of light.

He wasn't Spiderman. He was no hero. He couldn't take it anymore and wished he could have seen Angel one more time. A broken promise to his mother frenzied his memory.

He mumbled, "I'm sorry."

His muscles tensed as he prepared to pull the knife across his wrist. He stopped. Something or someone was coming toward him. Lance glanced up, distracted by the sounds of people crashing through the woods. Their approach echoed like a stampede, filled with chattering and laughing.

To do what he wanted required solitude, not an audience. He didn't want anyone to find him. He closed his knife, slid it into his pocket, wiped his sleeve against his eyes, and rubbed away the trickle of blood. When they were gone he would finish.

Four boys charged through the woods and moved toward Lance oblivious to the possibility someone else may be near. From their appearance, they were surfers and also carried a six-pack of beer. Both items roused a momentary interest.

They hadn't noticed him and nearly stumbled on Lance.

"Hey," Lance greeted.

All four boys screamed and stumbled. Walter lurched backward and fell down. Fearful, Pug and Steve backed away together, doing a type of jitterbug to escape from what they still couldn't see.

Startled, Brent held his spot. "Man, you scared the crud out of me."

They had no way of knowing what they just prevented. The knife was about to fall out of Lance's pocket, but he managed to shove it back in. He flashed them a wiry grin.

"Sorry."

Walter crawled to his feet while Brent extended his hand. "Hi, I'm Brent Baughman." He pointed to the one who had fallen down. "And this is Walter Hester." He pointed to the two boys who were letting go of each other. "That's Steve Boyd and the tall one is Pug Jennings."

"Lance Renfro," responded Lance as he surveyed them closely and sized them up. Brent was slightly taller with a muscular frame, an athletic type but with the same bronze tan and brown streaks in his hair from obvious time in the sun. Walter was a copy of them, but about four inches shorter with wavy brown hair. Pug was short and stocky with a flat nose similar to a fighter. Steve was tall and lanky.

The thing that drew Lance to them was their hair. Long locks hung slightly over their ears, almost as long as his. The four were not jocks. They were the kind Lance preferred to hang out with.

"From around here?" Brent asked.

"Nope. Just moved here from California."

Walter's eyes perked up. "California?"

Pug surveyed Lance. "Surfer?"

"Yeah."

Brent pulled out a beer and shoved it toward Lance. "Wanna brewski?"

"Sure."

Brent tossed Lance one of the beers.

"What are ya'll doing here?" said Lance.

With a shrug Brent exclaimed, "Going to the swing. Wanna come?"

New Friends

***

Buffalo Bayou was dark and dangerous. Still the boys plodded ahead with only the moon and stars to guide them. They reached a spot where a tree had fallen across the bayou and prepared to cross. After a dangerous balancing act they reached the other side. Steve almost fell in, but managed to grab a thick branch tilting at a slight angle. Otherwise he would have been in the water with the fish and only God knew what else. Once all five were safely across, they took a moment to chug from their beers. All kinds of creatures scampered through the brush and away from the five boys.

The oak tree was tall and a rope dangled from a long thick branch. A thin leader line hung from the bottom of the thick rope and was tied to a gangly tree on the bank. Brent untied the smaller one and proceeded to pull the larger rope toward the bank.

He was the first to swing across. They continued to swing and drink and be guys. A half hour later they were fairly inebriated.

Pug decided to show his prowess. "Watch this."

With the rope in his hand he ran parallel to the bank until the rope jerked him from his feet. Instead of swinging directly across in a straight line and coming back, he made a sweeping arc that would have turned into a complete circle, except for the fact he plowed into the bank. With a sickening thud he crashed and let out a drunken groan, then let go of the rope and rolled down the bank.

The other four, laughing, staggered to his side. Pug smashed his foot into the exposed root of an old oak tree, almost taking off his toenail. He ripped off part of his T-shirt and wrapped his foot. They were all going to walk him out, but he didn't want to interrupt their fun. Steve volunteered to take him home.

Brent, Walter, and Lance remained behind and continued to swing. A while later Walter wobbled drunkenly and finally fell down.

Sprawled on the bank, Brent scrutinized Walter, laughed, and took another sip of his beer. He turned toward Lance. "So you'll be going to Lee with us?"

"Yeah."

"Wanna see our surfboards?"

"Sure."

Brent shook Walter, but all he did was moan. "Walter. Walter?"

Lance waved his hand in the air. "Man, he's wasted."

How they managed to get out of the bayou and arrive at their respective houses was still a little of a mystery, but they did manage to do it without falling into the water.

***

Filled with tools, Brent's garage was a virtual workshop. Two surfboards stretched across a pair of sawhorses. Brent and Walter beamed while Lance inspected their surfboards. He rubbed his hands along the boards and his face brightened. Next to them was a '65 red and white Volkswagen camper covered with stickers. The van still appeared new.

Walter asked, "You surfed Malibu?"

Lance nodded, "Yeah." He backed away from the boards and shook his head. "These are longboards. No good."

"What do you mean?" said Brent. "They're California boards. Everyone here uses longboards."

"For California they're okay. How high are your waves here?"

Walter held his hand to his waist. "Three maybe five feet."

"Have trouble working them?"

"A little," said Brent.

"The bigger the wave, the more you can do?"

Walter and Brent nodded, curious as to where Lance was taking the questions.

"You don't need a big gun for ankle-breakers. A shorter board is easier to maneuver. Better for small waves."

Brent said, "So where do we get some?"

Lance grinned, "I can make 'em." He frowned and shrugged. "But I don't have a place to work on 'em."

A smile slowly filled Brent's face as he waved his arms around his garage. "You do now."

***

Lance worked on three short surfboards. Brent and Walter helped with the construction. On the workbench sat an eleven-inch black and white G.E. television. Brent took a break to turn on and tune in the small television. He twisted the antenna but with little results other than static while the vertical and horizontal continued to twitch in all directions.

Frustrated he said, "Hey, Walter can you fix this and get the rabbit ears to work?"

Walter laid down the sand paper and hastened to Brent's aid. Brent was all too happy to move aside and let Walter work his magic. Walter twisted the antenna until the picture came in vertically. Then he fine-tuned the horizontal and was greeted to a man jumping up and down on a car. The sign overhead read "Art Grindle."

The salesman-owner jumped up and down on the hood of an old Dodge as he yelled, "Iwantasellyouacar! Only five-hundred dollars today."

While Brent watched and chuckled, Lance wiped off his hands and chuckled, "That guy is crazy."

Brent nodded, "Yeah, Art Grindle is a nut case but he sells cars."

About that time the grill of the Dodge fell off, and without a moment's hesitation Grindle ripped the five hundred dollar sign in half. "Make that two-fifty. Come on down to 5725 Westheimer right now! We have the car of your dreams."

The commercial ended leaving all three shaking their heads and laughing. Brent and Walter's favorite program, Star Trek continued. While Spock talked to Captain Kirk Lance stopped and watched.

Spock said, "Save her, do as your heart tells you to do, and millions will die who did not die before."

Lance pointed at Spock, "Think it will ever be like that?"

Brent pointed at Walter, "Ask Mr. Wizard."

Walter made a face at Brent. "That futuristic stuff is going to happen. In the next few years, we'll even walk on the moon."

Lance and Brent chuckled.

"That was Kennedy's dream," said Lance. "And he's dead."

Brent motioned to Walter, "Go ahead, tell him the rest."

This was Walter's world. He was confident when he spoke. "Similar to Star Trek, we'll have communicators that will be comparable to telephones, but with moving pictures."

Lance interrupted, "You've been reading too much Dick Tracy. My dad had a stereo with a dozen tubes and half of them were as big as a banana. How you going to wear that on your wrist?" He pointed at the portable television. "… With a television screen like that?"

"No, really. We'll all have telephones in our pockets and computers as little as transistors. They won't use tubes, and television screens will be no bigger than the cover of your watch."

Again, Brent and Lance chuckled.

Walter tried to defend himself. "Really. IBM has something that looks similar to a postcard, but with many holes that store information and maybe one day even songs. It will happen."

"Come on. That's only science fiction. Really?" said Lance.

Walter nodded his head enthusiastically.

Lance could not conceive such an advanced world and shook his head in disbelief. "Not in our lifetime."

***

During the day they worked on the boards and at night Walter and Brent felt it their obligation to show Lance around Houston. Their main hangouts were the Catacombs on Post Oak near Westheimer and La Maison on Richmond in the Montrose area. But Lance was also introduced to Alan's Landing in downtown Houston and Old Market Square where local bands played their new songs. Places like La Bastille, Love Street and the Cellar were frequented by people like Liza Minnelli. The Coastliners—dubbed "The Gulf Coast Beach Boys"—showcased Tommy Meekins and Ozzie Hart as they belted out *Alright*. The 13th Elevators performed their rock and roll songs while Fever Tree, the psychedelic rock band of the 1960s, played their classic *San Franciscan Girls*.

Despite all this action, the boys always seemed to gravitate to the Catacombs. It was close to home and bands from Lee and Lamar performed frequently.

They managed to catch a few summer movie releases at the Majestic and Metropolitan theaters downtown but they dreaded the long lines and tended to gravitate to the local Windsor Theater at Richmond and Loop 610 near where they lived. The last movie they watched was *To Sir With*

Love with Sidney Poitier and a young kid, Christian Roberts. Although Lance disagreed both Brent and Walter thought Lance was a lot like Roberts. While Walter drooled over Lulu and even bought the cassette so he could hear her sing the title song, Brent noticed how Sidney Poitier reminded him of Lee's Coach Turner.

Only a few weeks had passed before Lance finished the new boards. Grinning ear to ear, he stood behind Brent and Walter as they admired his craftsmanship. Excited, they turned to Lance and nodded their approval.

Brent said, "Awesome."

Walter agreed. "Cherry."

Brent stared at Lance's board and eyebrows wrinkled when he saw the number "43" beautifully detailed and embedded in the middle near the tip. "What's the number forty-three for?"

For a moment Lance was stunned. He shook it off and said, "Nothing. Just an old memory."

Walter chuckled, "Like a good luck charm."

Lance stared at the number and snickered, "Yeah. He stared at the number, "A good luck charm."

Brent rubbed over the number with his fingers. "Looks like you carved it with a kni9fe and then filled it in with epoxy."

"Yeah, that's exactly what I did."

Brent added, "That is some great work."

Walther chimed in, "Yeah it's beautiful."

"Thanks." Lance quickly changed the subject, "Only one more week until school, so let's hit the surf. I hear Surfside is the best."

The enthusiasm on the faces of both boys disappeared instantly.

Walter was actually somewhat afraid. "No! We go to Galveston."

"Brown and his guys are at Surfside." Brent added, "It's their hangout."

"Who's Brown?" Lance asked.

"Jim Brown, our school's quarterback. He and the rest of the team rule the beach at Surfside."

For a moment Lance flashed a bit of anger and gritted his teeth. "If he's like most jocks, he parades the beach. He doesn't attack the waves. One thing for sure—he doesn't own the beach."

Stunned, Brent and Walter glanced at each other. Both chuckled nervously.

Walter said, "You're a wild man, Lance."

"Naw, Walter. I just do what I want." He grinned at his two friends, "Surfside."

Stunned, Brent and Walter stared at each other, but slowly grinned. They turned to Lance, held back for a moment, and in unison yelled, "Surfside!"

Chapter 4
SURFSIDE

On their way to Surfside, Brent drove the Volkswagen van while Walter sat in the passenger seat and Lance lounged in the back.

Walter warned Lance, "Avoid Brown. He's a pain in the ass. Unfortunately, he's the best quarterback in the state. We're currently picked to win state this year, too."

"Must be good," said Lance.

Brent grunted. "Yeah, he's good and he knows it."

"He sounds like a jerk."

Bitterness filled Walter's words, "Just a bully."

The other two didn't notice Lance when his hands clenched to fists. A momentary surge of anger lit his eyes.

"I know his kind," said Lance through gritted teeth. But just as rapidly his anger vanished.

Brent turned to Lance. "One more thing. Stay away from Dawn."

"Dawn?"

"Brown's girlfriend. She's got his senior ring. They're going steady."

***

High school students packed Surfside for the final week before school started. Cars lined the beach and surfers rode the waves. Near the jetties lingered a group of well-to-do teenagers who made preparations for the day. Despite the heat, they proudly wore their "Robert E. Lee Generals" letterman jackets as a symbol of their status.

From exceptionally prestigious families, the cars they parked were expensive. One of the boys bragged about the new Mustang his parents had bought him. It cost just over two thousand dollars. They had almost bought him a brand new Shelby 350 Mustang for more than twice that amount, but decided it was just too expensive.

Many of the boys had already taken the jackets off and prepared to enjoy a day in the surf, but they didn't give any indication they were surfers. A few tossed around a football and it was easy to see where they really excelled. Football was their sport, not surfing. An entourage pursued Jim Brown. Most hung on his every move. He would have been an excellent cult leader. Muscular and tanned, the quarterback appeared to be more of a body builder. But when he threw the football there was no doubt he was a quarterback.

Bigger and more muscular than Jim, Cotton Dickey, the Lee running back, stayed near. Bill Martin and Mike McClain hung on Jim's every word, as well. They were big but did not match Jim or Cotton for size. It was painfully amusing that the football players were more comfortable in the sand than in the surf. They tried, but they were so out of place in the water.

Cotton was a follower but appeared a little different than the rest. His curly blond hair gave no doubt as to where his nickname had come. Although he was a little timid and easily intimidated in Jim Brown's presence, he was a demon on the football field and a dependable friend.

While they tossed the football, the Lee cheerleaders set up covers between the cars and spread blankets beneath the hastily prepared shelters. Joyce Ann Miller hummed a tune while she worked. Many believed this brunette was the prettiest girl at Lee, perhaps even more popular than Dawn Alexander. With round blue eyes and a smooth brown complexion with natural red lips, the boys all vied for her affection. She shunned them one and all, including the football players. Most of the jocose dreamed of Joyce Ann wearing their senior ring around her neck. Yet her neck remained bare, and the reasons stymied the players.

The most charming thing about Joyce Ann was her personality. She always smiled and appeared to be happy. No one had ever seen her angry and she was fun to be around.

Next to Joyce Ann were Denise Collins and Sue King, who busily pulled things from the car. Denise helped with an unstoppable energy. She had no current boyfriend, but it wasn't that other boys hadn't tried or didn't want her. She was fond of them all and enjoyed tormenting each and every one, changing boyfriends about as frequently as a new football game came around. Undaunted, every boy hoped and prayed he'd be "the one," but after two years of high school many lost hope. With light brown hair, her beauty rivaled that of Joyce Ann.

Sue took cookies, drinks, and snacks from a few assorted brown paper bags. A blanket was spread between a blue and white, '67 Chevrolet SS Impala, and Brown's red '67 Corvette Stingray. A natural blond with a beautiful figure, Sue was definitely another Lee beauty and won Most Beautiful in her junior year, which took place before Joyce Ann had transferred from another school. She also had no ring, perhaps because many considered her to be dingy. Still, there were boys all over school who wanted her to be their girlfriend. Rumors said she did have a steady, but he attended another school. Mostly she hung out with the other cheerleaders, and especially Dawn and Jim.

The other cheerleader, Dawn Alexander, dug a hole for the fire. She wasn't a classic beauty like the rest, but there was something about her that attracted the boys like a magnet. Her naturally wavy brown head of hair had a bounce that matched her personality. Although her attributes were desirable, it was her eyes that set her apart from other girls—two mystical light blue pools of life that an unwary young man might just drown in. Her eyes could disarm anyone, as if she could look right through your soul. With boundless energy and a quick wit everyone loved, she was always pleasant and fun to be around. When things were critical, she was the one you could always count on and know when she said it would be done, it would be done.

Seldom did anyone see that fiery side of Dawn's personality, considering she loved to help others and was a true and loyal friend to all who crossed her path. But she could be spitfire. Oh yes, she could.

Dawn's best friend through childhood, Marilyn Tacconelly, helped alongside on the beach as well. She wasn't the most striking girl at first sight, not for lack of beauty, but rather because of the way she dressed. Her hair was never fully fixed and the oddly shaped glasses took away from a hidden treasure. Marilyn was a little awkward but once people got to know her personality, that became her real splendor. She was shy—or more accurately—intimidated in the presence of the cheerleaders and jocks. Jim Brown especially intimidated her.

Afraid to venture away, Marilyn leaned against Dawn's car as though it was some type of security. She failed to see her inner beauty, but her best friends Dawn and Cotton certainly recognized it. Cotton stood near Marilyn and talked to her in more than a friendly manner. He saw underneath the shyness and glasses, knowing her better than anyone other than Dawn.

Everyone liked Marilyn except Jim Brown. He disliked having her anywhere he went, especially the beach. The problem was she was best friends with his girlfriend Dawn. He continued to glance in her direction and noticed her playfully clinging to Dawn. The more he noticed, the angrier he became until he reached his limit. Jim stopped tossing the football and walked straight through the other girls until he reached Dawn, who was discussing Monday's cheerleader practice with Sue, Denise, and Joyce Ann. Mike and Bill clung to Jim somewhat akin to pet dogs.

While some of the players grabbed their boards and charged into the small waves, Jim continued to stare at Cotton and Marilyn. Still, Cotton continued his friendly exchange with Marilyn.

Disgusted, Jim turned to Dawn and pointed rudely. "Why do you always bring Miss Misfit?"

Seldom irritated, Dawn gave Jim a tart response. "Marilyn is my best friend."

With a grunt and a wave of disgust Jim said, "Never mind."

Defensive, Dawn retaliated. "Marilyn, and I are gonna walk out the jetty."

Again, Jim waved Dawn away. "Whatever. We're gonna hit the surf."

He turned to Bill and Mike. "Let's go."

Resembling happy puppies, Bill and Mike followed Jim. Others blindly trailed their leader into the surf while Dawn plodded through the sand toward Marilyn.

Chapter 5

LIVE FOR TODAY

Surfside Beach was nearly filled to capacity when Brent pulled his Volkswagen camper van along the water's edge, hunting for an empty spot. A car pulled away and left an opening within a few car spaces from the "Generals" gang, and just a few yards shy of the tall sand dunes.

This was considered "no man's land" to surfers. Lance convinced them to pull in anyway and Brent maneuvered his van into the vacant space. Lance, Brent, and Walter bailed out and unfastened their boards which they laid in the sand. Then each took a bar of wax and rubbed the walking surface to assure a better grip with their feet.

While they waxed the boards, Denise, Joyce Ann, and Sue walked past. Joyce Ann eyed Brent.

Lance made sure to take time to eye the girls. "Who are the beach bunnies?"

Brent said, "Cheerleaders from Lee."

"Choice babes. Maybe school won't be so bad," commented Lance with a grin.

Brent shook a bar of wax at Lance. "Say that after Brown sees you talking with them."

"Bummer." Lance pointed to the jetties. "What's that?"

Walter said, "The jetties."

"Tanker ships come through there. It's about a half mile wide," Brent added. "The jetties extend out about a mile into the gulf."

Lance unsuccessfully tried to peer further. "What's on the other side?"

"Quintana."

Curiosity had the best of Lance. "I'm gonna check it out."

Brent nodded toward Brown and the team. "Stay away from them. Brown's a real badass."

"Hey man, don't sweat it." Lance stared at Brown. "He doesn't look like a surfer."

Brent shook his head in disgust. "Goes in the water, shows off his muscles and hangs out on the beach."

Lance grinned. "Are the guys clinging to him football players, or just Gremlins?"

"Both," answered Brent. With a quick glance and an understanding smirk, he added, "Yeah, just a bunch of grommets."

Lance laughed.

Suddenly, Brent was sincere. "Listen Lance, I'm serious. Stay away from them, especially Brown," he warned once again.

Lance snickered. "He's a hodad."

Brent chuckled, glanced at Brown, and grinned knowingly at Lance. "Yeah. A hodad."

***

A concrete walkway separated the beach from the channel and was lined with concrete riprap. Across the channel a similar jetty separated Surfside from Quintana. The channel provided a calm recess where huge tankers and other ships gained access to the port. Both sides were lined the entire way with boulders and concrete riprap. Lance stood on one of the boulders and peered to the far side.

From a distant radio on the beach, the Grassroots song *Let's Live for Today* drifted to the jetties where Lance contemplated the half-mile swim to Quintana—a swim not imperative, but simply desired due to its existence. He listened to the song and tossed a flat stone in the air, then caught it.

While Lance contemplated the swim Dawn and Marilyn bounced joyfully along the jetty on their return from the far end. They were almost upon him when Dawn spotted him staring across the channel.

Out of curiosity she smirked and asked, "Thinking about diving in?"

With his eyes still fixed on Quintana, Lance skipped the stone across the water, "Nope. Swimming across."

Somewhat surprised, she said, "That's crazy. No one swims the channel."

Confidence echoed from his words. "I can." He turned to face Dawn, and for a moment remembered himself at the swing with Angel. Dawn flashed a disarming smile and words failed him. He shook the thought from his mind and managed to grin back. She wasn't like Angel, who had blonde curly hair. This girl was a brunette.

Dawn peered across the channel, "You'd need a lot of faith to swim across."

There was the word *faith* again; however, it didn't sound as bad coming from her as it did from the minister or his old coach. He pointed across to the other side. "Faith won't get me across this channel." He turned back to Dawn. "My ability will get me across."

She grunted and challenged him. "So what do you do besides thinking about swimming to your death?"

He shrugged his broad shoulders. "I… " He heard the song and said, "Live for today."

Dawn laughed, rolled her head and returned her gaze to Lance, "Don't you worry about tomorrow, the future?"

Brooding, Lance replied, "People worry too much about tomorrow. I don't anymore."

Marilyn grunted and poked Dawn. "What a rebel. He probably rides a motorcycle!"

Lance snickered to Marilyn, "Honda." He jumped gracefully to the concrete walk and came face to face with Dawn, then extended his hand. "Lance Renfro." Again his attention returned to fading images of Angel as a faraway voice said, "Ang… "

"Dawn Alexander," she said as she took Lance's hand firmly. She nodded to her friend. "This is Marilyn."

Lance appeared a little disappointed and Dawn was quick to notice. "Are you okay?"

Lance snapped out of his trance and managed a roguish grin. "So, you're Dawn. I hear you go to Lee."

Curious, she asked, "How do you know so much about me?"

"I was told you're dangerous to hang around."

"Who told you that?"

"Friends."

Marilyn whispered in Dawn's ear, "They must have warned him about Jim."

Lance grinned and nodded his head.

Dawn laughed mischievously. "Well, I can talk to whoever I want. Jim doesn't own me."

Marilyn wasn't as confident. "If Jim sees us, you know what he'll do."

"You telling me it will be safer to swim the channel?" Lance smirked, "What about tomorrow?"

Dawn giggled and rolled her eyes. "That's not funny."

This time Marilyn snickered, "Well, it's a good thing he lives for today, because if Jim finds out, there might not be any tomorrow."

Marilyn's comment surprised Dawn. "Marilyn!" she chided.

***

Lance, Marilyn, and Dawn walked along the beach together and occasionally Lance and Dawn would brush their arms and hands against each other. Neither appeared to mind, nor did they avoid the contact. When they neared the others the two girls excused themselves to use the restroom and turned off in another direction.

Taking his time Lance meandered back to the van and his friends. There he discovered that Brent and Walter had already taken to the water. Shielding his eyes with his hands, he searched the waves until he spotted his friends on their new surfboards, bobbing like corks in the water and patiently waiting for the right wave.

He picked up his board and prepared to charge the waves with his friends, then hesitated. Again he peered out to the waters of the gulf and searched far beyond his friends. He loved the sounds of the waves crashing to shore. The ocean was always special and alluring, and once again mysteriously beckoned him.

Taking time to anchor his board vertically in the sand, he walked deliberately toward the water and waded out. He wouldn't be surfboarding. He would be swimming. The sand pulled at his feet and the waves tried to push him back towards shore. Both seemed to be nature's warnings of the dangers beyond.

Were the sand and waves trying to protect him… or hold him back from some greater reward? Everyone he knew had always been afraid to take that next step. The unknown was right in front of him and the unseen lurked in the waters below.

He continued in a dream-like state until he could no longer keep his head above water. Safety was gone, but he was also released from the restraints holding him back. This day was no different than the others, and he continued alone knowing others would be too afraid to follow. Using the breast stroke, he continued until he reached Brent and Walter floating on their new surfboards waiting patiently for a wave.

Brent was the first to see Lance. "Hey man, where's your board?"

"Next to your van," said Lance. He continued to float next to them.

"You better get it and come back out," said Walter.

"Later," said Lance. "I want to swim out a little farther first."

"It's too deep and you have no board. Are you crazy?" said Brent.

With a smirk and a mischievous grin Lance said, "Probably."

The boys shook their heads as they watched Lance create an increasing distance between him and the safe shore line.

Lance continued stroking until he reached the point he sought. No longer could he hear the noise of the waves crashing on the beach or the yells of the surfers and beach goers. Quiet, peace and slightly eerie noises encompassed his being. This was his place and he knew it well: solitude. Here was a tranquility that words could not describe. This location was now special and felt as though it belonged to only him. The waves rose high and dipped back gently into a valley. Each time he would float to the top and back down in a repetitive, yet comforting, manner.

It was as if he was being cradled. The rhythmic ocean continued to hold Lance in a gentle and pleasing serenity. A sizeable wave approached, and as he began to rise to the top a few little fish darted through the salt water's surface. A mullet frantically leaped from the wave and wiggled in the air before slicing back into the ocean. Lance felt something brush his leg and noticed it felt bigger than a fish, yet he still felt no fear. He drifted at peace with everything around him.

Content, he decided to embark on a return to reality. But after swimming for a short time it was apparent he was not making progress. The aggressive current continued to pull him farther from shore. In similar situations others might panic and try desperately to swim until they were exhausted. Each and every year swimmers perished from the exact same thing along the Texas coast.

It had happened to him before, and Lance understood the ocean. He knew there was nothing he could do and was captive to the mercy of the currents. For his own safety, he didn't fight it. The ocean had him in its gentle grasp, leading him where it wanted. He had reached an emotional point of joy and enjoyed the pleasing peace. He was willing and happy to let the currents control him. He kept his body relaxed. There was no way of knowing how long the ocean would pull him along, but he knew it would eventually end and the thought of that inevitable finale saddened him.

Then ever so slightly, he felt the ocean release its hold. Serenely, Lance began to breast stroke towards shore. A few minutes later he was making progress and it wasn't long before he reached a location far off from his intended destination. The current had pulled him down the beach about a half mile from his friends. Upon his exit from oblivion he appeared no worse physically than if he had been on a leisure walk down the beach. If anything, he was more relaxed and at peace with the world that surrounded him. Casually he trekked back to the van and his board, ready to surf the Texas waves.

***

Enthralled at their abilities, everyone on shore continued to observe Brent, Walter and Lance surf the waves. Even the experienced surfers were impressed with their ability to maneuver with such ease. The short boards worked the waters magically. Even so, most of what they did was from their natural ability in the water, especially Lance.

Dawn and Marilyn gazed at the three surfers with more than just casual interest.

Jim, Cotton, Mike and Bill also kept an interested eye on the three surfers as they ruled the surf. Jealousy consumed Jim when he noticed Dawn watching Lance. He hunted for something or someone to torment when his gaze fell on Marilyn. He immediately glared at the poor girl and became irate

"I don't know why Dawn hangs out with that spaz," he said to Cotton.

The smile disappeared from Cotton's face. Jim's comment came from nowhere and stunned him. Afraid of Jim's reaction, he still tried to defend Marilyn. "Marilyn is nice once you get to know her."

Jim furrowed his eyes. "Not you too." Jim shook his head, threw his hands up and groaned in disgust. "You're hopeless, Cotton."

Everyone continued to admire the ability of Brent and Lance in the surf.

Mike McClain said, "Those guys are awesome."

Even Bill Martin marveled at their ability. "Yeah, man. Off the Richter."

With an air of arrogance Jim stuck his nose in the air. "Well they better stick to surfing, 'cause I'm gonna break the first one who talks to Dawn." He turned to Bill and Mike. "Hey, let's toss the ball." He turned toward Cotton and barked orders. "Cotton, get the ball."

Cotton ran to his car to retrieve the football.

Bill asked Jim, "You make out much with Dawn?"

"Make out? Man, I've gone all the way with Dawn."

Mike was stunned and wanted to know more, "No way. Not Dawn!"

"I've scored with her a bunch of times. I can't keep her away from me."

Abruptly, the conversation ended when Cotton arrived with the ball and tossed it to Jim.

Soon more than a dozen jocks started throwing the football around on the sandy beach. Jim was accurate with his tosses, hitting the mark every time.

While they threw the ball Lance made his final ride to the beach. He jumped off his board and let it trail behind. Just as next wave pushed the board, almost hitting his ankle, he stepped on the nose with his heel, shoved it underwater and allowed the following wave to knock the board almost vertical. Without a glance back Lance grabbed the board in style.

A few witnessed the unusual and difficult maneuver, including Cotton who said, "Man that was an awesome pearl. Did you see that?"

Lance came out of the water, laid his board down and walked straight for Dawn. She was alarmed and her lips formed the words, "NO, GO AWAY."

Lance moved intentionally in her direction.

When Jim saw Lance stroll toward Dawn his face filled with rage. He squeezed the football in anger, then an evil smile filled his face. He had plans for this newcomer. He fired the ball in Lance's direction as he yelled, "Hey dork! Think fast!"

Lance turned just in time to snatch the rocket from the air. There were some "Wows!" He glared at Jim with eyes of fire while clenching his fist. The familiar uncontrollable rage had returned.

Jim didn't notice because he was just as angry. "That chick's mine. Leave her alone."

Lance turned his head and grinned at Dawn, which only infuriated Jim even more. Slowly he turned his gaze back to Jim. "That chick? Hey dork, her name is Dawn."

A collective gasp emitted from the players and surfers who had gathered to observe this dramatic event. Most of the surfers knew Jim

Brown's hostile attitude, and laughs were abundant at Lance's words. None of the guys really enjoyed being around Jim, although in order to be popular it was a requirement. Secretly they reveled in the challenge offered up from this strange new surfer.

"Dawn's my girl. Stay away."

"Funny, I don't see your brand," said Lance with a smirk. "Double zero, isn't it?"

A few more chuckled, but most knew this new guy on the beach was doomed.

Lance spun the football on the end of his finger and grinned defiantly. It appeared he knew how to handle a football. "Nice ball. I bet saltwater is tough on the leather."

"You better not if you know what's good for you," Jim threatened.

With a smirk Lance glanced at the ball and spun it again in his hand. He smiled at Jim, took the football and held it as though he was about to throw. He brought his arm back as if he were a quarterback, then launched the ball deep into the saltwater. Everyone was shocked.

Lance grinned at Jim. "Fetch, Rover."

More onlookers laughed, but the laughter was mingled with gasps of disbelief as all eyes turned to Jim. He was livid. They all knew the football players were about to pulverize this bronze surfer full of clever retorts.

Even Jim gasped. "You turd!"

To everybody's amazement, Lance laughed at Jim. "You must be amazing in English class with that vocabulary."

Astonished at Lance's boldness, Dawn's concern was Jim's anger and what he would do to this strange surfer who obviously only *lived for today*. She remembered Marilyn's words that there might not be any tomorrow. How true, especially if Jim and the rest of the football team managed to get their hands on this bold newcomer. Dawn watched as things began to unravel before her.

Jim turned to his teammates and waved his arm at Lance. "Get him!"

A dozen of the jocks, along with Jim, charged through the sand. Only Cotton held back. Those on the beach were sure Lance was about to take his last breath.

The football team was stunned when Lance charged them. He bent low and growled just before he reached them. The players momentarily froze. This had never happened before. Unusual behavior was not what they expected and their slight hesitation gave Lance the precious seconds he needed as he streaked through the crowd untouched. Once safely on the other side of the angry mob, he laughed out loud as he continued to put distance between them.

Jim yelled, "Get him!"

Again, all the players charged after Lance. This time they wouldn't stop, which Lance counted on. He ran straight for the water and the jocks continued relentlessly in their pursuit. This strategy was intentional, for Lance wanted them to pursue him into the water. A moment later he slowed. Just as Jim and the players owned the football field, Lance owned the water.

From the beach Marilyn, Joyce Ann, Denise, Sue, Cotton, Dawn, Brent, and Walter could only observe. They were too shocked to help and too curious to stop watching what they believed to be a tragic event about to unfold before their eyes.

Incredulous, Dawn said, "He wants them to chase him. Is he crazy?"

Cotton said, "Man, those are not guys to mess around with."

In the water Lance's pace was steady and he kept the football players close. He waded out waist deep and stopped abruptly. With a grin on his face, he turned to face his pursuers.

Cotton continued to watch and unconsciously put his arm around Marilyn, which for a moment revealed his true feelings. Marilyn's eyes betrayed her, but she whispered, "Not here, Cotton." So there would be no misunderstanding, she added the warning, "Jim."

Unaware and surprised at what he had done, Cotton pulled his arm away.

Not far away, Brent and Walter could only wait to see the outcome, not so much afraid but rather wishing it had been them who had challenged Jim and the whole football team.

Concerned, Brent mumbled, "Man, they're gonna kill him."

Dawn had the same premonition. "Oh, God! Somebody help him."

Clueless, Sue said, "Jim doesn't need any help."

More than a dozen jocks closed in on Lance. This time they formed a semi-circle so he couldn't escape. One reached for Lance, but pulled back when Lance screamed.

"Let go!" Lance shrieked. He jerked around as though some unseen creature had his leg and cast a terrified look down to where "something" had grabbed him. He managed to look at the football player next to him. Fear and terror filled his eyes. Suddenly, Lance appeared to be yanked beneath the water. The jocks jumped back. They searched the water but found no sign of Lance. Terrified, most were already treading quickly toward the beach and the security of the beach.

Dawn and Cotton were horrified with the intense belief and fear that something had taken Lance hostage. Others wondered what was worse—the unseen denizens of the deep or Jim Brown. They all knew Jim, and no one wanted to face him one-on-one, let alone with the whole football team at his command.

Brent and Walter were more suspicious than terrified. They knew the water.

Suddenly, a jock was pulled under. When he surfaced, he screamed in horror and continued to scream as he splashed frantically back to the beach. Before anyone could move Bill was pulled under with the same results. When he surfaced he gasped for air while chocking on a mouthful of disgusting salt water.

Still there was no Lance.

Now wild with terror, half of them charged back to the beach. Mike moved as fast as he could through the water toward the sandy shore, but he was unable to get far. Something beneath the water jerked him to a stop and he barely managed a blood-curdling shriek before he went under. Everyone on the beach was horrified. A moment later, Mike popped to the surface gasping and chocking for air while splashing hysterically.

Now everyone tried to escape the unseen creature. None of the players remained in the water when Lance finally surfaced for air. He laughed and pointed at the players on the beach who had all run away, exactly as he had anticipated.

Enraged, Jim pointed and roared, "There he is!"

Relieved, Dawn laughed. Brent and Walter understood what Lance had just accomplished against Lee's awesome football jocks and were hysterical.

Cotton mumbled, "I can't believe it," as he and Marilyn laughed out loud.

Marilyn said, "How funny… and to Jim, of all people!" She continued to giggle.

Only some of the jocks who had fled to the beach dared to return and help Jim. Even though it was obvious Lance had pulled a successful trick on the whole team, the boys were still visibly shaken from the unseen monster beneath the ocean's surface. The beach was full of cowards.

Lance managed to laugh as they charged him again. He gulped a chest full of air and disappeared beneath the water one more time.

All the jocks stopped where they were. They waited for a moment. Another jock screamed and was pulled beneath the water. Lance continued his pursuit. He surfaced momentarily only to disappear again.

On the beach stood Brent, Walter, Marilyn, Dawn and Cotton where they continued to laugh at Lance's antics. It was a full-blown comedy, and no longer were they concerned for his safety. This was fun and they enjoyed what he was doing to the football team, helpless in the water against this lone assailant.

Lance continued to pull them down one by one. There was a reason for his madness. Each time he surfaced he came a little bit closer to Jim.

Finally it was Jim who disappeared beneath the water!

Cotton was alarmed. "Oh, man! Jim's gonna be pissed."

Coughing and chocking, Jim popped to the surface. So did Lance, but this time just behind Jim. Lance stuck his arm past Jim's shoulder and pointed.

Lance said, "There he is! Get him!"

Since all Jim could see was an arm, Jim screamed out in rage and plunged forward as instructed. Behind Jim, Lance pointed and yelled again, "In front of you, Jimbo!"

Jim hesitated and saw the other jocks. They all stared at the person behind him. Some even pointed. Jim turned to see Lance who had a grin stretched across his face.

"Stick to football. Swimming isn't your bag."

Jim screamed and lunged at Lance, but he grabbed nothing. Lance was gone again. The jocks moved very slowly toward Jim. They searched and searched, but Lance was gone.

Near the beach Lance finally surfaced. He laughed victoriously and waved to Jim and the other jocks in the water. Mimicking Jim the best he could, Lance pointed at himself with both hands and yelled, "Here he is. Get him!" He laughed uncontrollably.

Many more laughed, which irritated Jim immensely. He pointed at Lance and repetitively let out, "Get him!"

This time on solid ground, the jocks on the beach were filled with confidence and began to slowly march toward Lance, who glanced past them to Brent and Walter. Lance was cut off and couldn't make it back out to the water. He knew they wouldn't fall for his trick a second time and gazed toward the jetty. It was his only chance.

Jim struggled as he exited the water and walked toward Lance. Now he was confident the troublemaker was in his grasp. "He's mine. Okay, candy ass, let's see what you got."

A dozen of the Jocks moved in as Jim led the charge.

Lance turned back to the jetty. In the distance a tanker blew its horn. Lance turned a defiant smile to his pursuers as though he knew something they didn't and yelled, "Catch me if you can." Instantly, he spun about to face the jetty.

Once again the jocks were caught with their pants down. They never expected him to run toward the jetty.

Abruptly Dawn, Brent, and Walter understood as they saw Lance take off.

Dawn mumbled, "Don't."

Walter said, "Oh, man, he's screwed."

Lance ran hard toward the jetty with Jim and the jocks in hot pursuit.

Concerned, Cotton said, "He's dead meat."

Curiosity and maybe even the urge to save Lance pulled everyone to the jetty. This would be a show like no other. Lance never slowed as he continued up the sand slope to the concrete walkway. In full stride he jumped from the jetty and disappeared from view.

Sure only a ghastly sight would greet those swiftly approaching the jetty. They continued on, for all knew that on the other side and below was nothing but sharp, rough, uneven boulders. There would be an injury as a reward for the gallant and costly jump.

Dawn gasped, "Oh, no!"

Cotton grabbed Marilyn. "You don't want to see this."

Still, the crowd continued to the top where Jim and the jocks had already stopped. People forced their way through.

Somehow Lance must have jumped from jagged boulder to jagged boulder, miraculously unscathed until he reached the water. Already fifty yards away, he stroked the water rapidly leaving behind a wake resembling a motorboat more than a person. The rhythmic strokes revealed the ability of a person who knew what he was doing. He didn't swim with fear, but rather intent purpose and sheer joy in his natural surroundings.

Mike McClain said, "He's nuts."

Cotton confirmed, "He's got some guts. I wouldn't challenge that ship."

Jim glanced at the tanker then back to Lance. He flashed a triumphant smile. "The tanker's gonna make mincemeat out of him."

Everyone watched the race with anticipation to see who or what would reign victorious: a bold surfer versus a steel framed ship.

Brent grabbed Walter and motioned with his head for them to go. As they ran for the van Brent said, "Grab Lance's board." He flashed a grin at Walter, "We're going to Quintana."

Walter was confused, "Why?"

Brent managed a smile as they ran, "To get Lance."

On the jetty, everyone continued to watch in morbid fascination. It appeared Lance was going to make it with plenty of time to spare. This made Jim sad, Dawn relieved and the witnesses entertained.

Bill Martin was awed at Lance's prowess in the water. "That guy can sure swim."

"Like a fish. He's bookin,'" agreed Cotton.

Irritated, Jim said, "Shut-up."

Dawn took a deep breath and let out a sigh of relief.

Lance beat the tanker and managed to climb to the top on the other side, even taking a moment to wave back to his pursuers. He relaxed and continued to wave until the tanker passed between them.

Much to Jim's dismay, most of the spectators cheered at Lance's triumph.

***

Lance ambled along the beach and kicked at the sand. The

Volkswagen van pulled up next to him. Brent stuck his head out the window while the radio, tuned to KILT, blared the Blues Magoo's *We Ain't Got Nothing Yet.*

Smugly Brent said, "Want a lift?"

Lance laughed, nodded and ran around to the passenger side. The door slid open and in he jumped. All three were excited at their new adventure and rapid-fire talk filled the air as Lance settled in the back seat.

Walter said, "Man, I've never seen anything like that."

Lance managed a laugh and relaxed. "To tell the truth, I haven't had that much fun in a long, long time. Man, that was a blast! Did you see Dawn?"

"Dawn is the least of your worries," Brent cautioned.

Walter chimed in, "No kidding. Jim is gonna kill you."

Brent chuckled, "What you did to Jim was awesome. But he's gonna pound your ass."

Lance waved it off, "Don't sweat it. Tell me more about Dawn."

Walter shook his head. "Messing with her will give you a short life expectancy."

Lance laughed.

Brent asked, "Why do you want to know about her?"

Lance shrugged and he let a momentary bit of happiness creep into his being. Happiness had become a rare thing, an extremely rare thing. "She reminds me of someone I knew." The brooding rebel returned, "But that was a long time ago."

He shifted his position in the back of the van and accidentally knocked some papers off the tiny sink just behind the driver's seat. He scrambled to pick them off the floor and noticed they were poems. He flipped through a few and saw Brent's signature at the bottom of each. "You wrote these?"

Brent checked the rearview mirror. Embarrassed, he reached back. "Give me those."

Lance pulled them away and continued to flip through. Brent had written about twenty poems and they were good. Lance locked on one called "The End" and began to read it out loud:

For the End, nothing would be the same.
This was the last play of the game.

"Hey don't read that," said Brent while reaching back in a desperate effort to retrieve his poems.

Walter smirked, "I didn't know you wrote poetry?"

"These are really good," said Lance.

"I want to hear it," said Walter. "Let him finish."

Reluctantly Brent gave in and concentrated on driving.

Lance continued:

For the End, nothing would be the same.
This was the last play of the game.

They needed four,
They had to score.

The quarterback said, "End, wide right.
Are you up for the fight?"

They came to the line,
For the very last time.

At the snap the End pushed hard,
And caught the defense off guard.

He ran with all his might,
His speed, such a sight.

He flew through the night,
To the flashes of light

Down the field spiraled the ball,
Too high, much too tall!

The End leaped for the sky.
His body so very, very high

Up, up even higher he did soar
As the frantic fans gave a thunderous roar.

The ball touched his fingertip.
He couldn't let it slip.

Another hand, it wasn't much.
Again, oh what a touch!

He gathered the ball in.
Touchdown--the End!

"Wow," said Lance. "You're good."
Red-faced, Brent managed, "It's nothing."
Walter grinned, "Why'd you write about a receiver?"

Brent shrugged his shoulders, "I've always wanted to play wide receiver. I've always wanted to catch a touchdown pass."

Walter nodded his head and smiled. "That's cool."

"Yeah," said Lance. He placed the poems back in the empty sink and sat back.

The radio disc jockey, Russ Knight, had a raspy voice much like Wolfman Jack. He spun a another record. "This is the Weird Beard, KILT. Hope you enjoyed the Magoos and now the number one song in the country…by the Doors, *Touch Me*."

Curious and excited Brent glanced at Walter and Lance. "You really liked them?"

In unison they said, "Yeah."

They drove on for a while before Brent checked the rearview mirror and nodded to Lance, "You got a job?"

"No."

"You do now."

"Doing what?"

Walter pulled some papers out of his pocket. "These guys all want short boards."

Lance took the papers. "I don't have a place to make them."

"My pad is your new office," said Brent.

Lance managed a grin, "Far out. I can use the dough."

***

That night Brent, Walter and Lance once again trekked to Buffalo Bayou and the swing. In hand were two six packs of beer. All three swung to their hearts content. They discussed and argued about the cheerleaders, surfing, new boards, Jim Brown, swimming the channel, but mostly the cheerleaders. After a few brewskis they were content to lounge along the bank and reminisce about the day's adventure.

Lance asked, "Where does Dawn live?"

"Stay away from her. Nobody messes with the cheerleaders," Brent warned.

Lance propped himself on his elbow. "So Dawn's a cheerleader?"

Walter said, "Yeah, Dawn, Sue, Joyce Ann and Denise."

Lance said, "I kinda like her."

Brent said, "Don't." To make his point he stood up and faced Lance, "Don't ever let Jim hear you say that. Let me give you a health warning—find another chick."

Chapter 6

ROBERT E. LEE GENERALS

The vacant lot across from the school was filled with cars. Students waited for the bell to start their school day.

The In-Crowd included many jocks. Jim, Cotton, Mike, Bill, Sue, Joyce Ann, Denise and Dawn were congregated next to Jim's Corvette and with them were three jocks who had not gone to the beach with the others. Ron, Marvin, and Will listened to the wild stories and heard first-hand about the new guy in town, Lance Renfro.

Farther down the lot was another group. Among them were Walter and Brent next to the VW van. Marilyn, Steve and Pug were with them. Pug wore a sandal on the foot he smashed while swinging at Buffalo Bayou. Bandages covered his toe.

Lance rumbled into the lot and pulled next to Brent.

From a distance Dawn twisted her neck to see Lance. Jim noticed, but before he could respond Dawn started to walk away. She turned to Jim, "I need to get something from Marilyn. See you in class."

He was furious and glared at Dawn for a moment, then turned and whispered to Mike and Bill. "We're gonna tear that dork apart."

The boys grinned and nodded in agreement.

As they navigated the parking lot Brent asked, "Ready for class?"

Lance folded his arms. "Nope."

The four boys chuckled as they walked toward the school. Pug limped as best he could to keep up with them.

Dawn continued her jog toward them and waved to Marilyn as she ran. "Marilyn!"

The boys turned at her voice and waited for her to catch up. She moved closer to Lance. For a moment they looked at each other eye-to-eye. Dawn glanced away, only to peek back.

They both said, "Hi."

Dawn glanced down then back up at Lance. "I've never seen anybody do what you did in the channel. That was an awful long way to swim."

"It wasn't that far."

They continued through the bulky steel doors guarding the school.

Marilyn said to Lance, "I can't believe the dive with all those concrete rocks."

He held his hand flat in front of him. "Just hit flat and don't go deep, otherwise you'll grind your face off."

Marilyn's mouth dropped in amazement, "Oh my goodness."

When they reached the main hall Pug and Steve went in the opposite direction. The others continued while Dawn and Lance dropped a little ways behind the others.

When they started up the stairs Dawn grabbed Lance and exclaimed, "Be careful. Jim wants you."

Brent, Marilyn, and Walter turned to listen while other students swarmed around them.

A mischievous grin lit up Lance's face. "Jim wants me? He's queer? Tell him he's not my type."

Brent and Walter chuckled. Again, Marilyn's mouth dropped open in disbelief.

Even Dawn was stunned and taken back. Furrows across her brow accented the gravity of her words, "I'm serious, Lance."

"Thanks for the warning."

Dawn gave a sigh of relief and beamed as she grabbed Marilyn and ran up the stairs.

Brent shook his head. "You must be on a suicide mission. Come on, we'll take you to the office so you can register."

They continued toward the office. Walter said, "Hey, you wanna play football?"

"Depends."

Brent said, "Sandlot, with a few other guys. We'll take you with us after school."

***

The bell rang and all the students poured from the classrooms to rush to their lockers and retrieve books. No one wanted to get caught in the halls when the bell signaled a tardy. Lance strolled to his locker to load books and snapped the combination lock shut. Then two things happened simultaneously: the one-minute warning bell rang and Jim came up from behind . He shoved Lance against the locker then spun him around. Not only was Jim facing him, but it appeared as though half the football team backed him.

The remaining students promptly dispersed. Only Jim with his entourage and Lance remained in the hall.

Jim snickered, "Not so tuff out of the water."

Lance turned his head to study the jocks. "Doesn't look like you are either. Hey Jimbo, you need these goons to take me?"

A few of the Jocks chuckled, which infuriated Jim. He smashed a fist into Lance's stomach. Lance gasped, dropped his books, doubled over and fell to his knees.

"Dawn's my girl! Stay away," yelled Jim. Angry and bent on getting his personal justice he jerked Lance to his feet and was about to finish when a voice echoed down the hall.

"Mr. Brown, do we have a situation here?" asked Principal Davis.

Everyone turned in alarm to see the Principal. The bald, rotund middle-aged man carried a three-foot long paddle with numerous holes to reinforce punishment. He saw Lance, turned to Jim and asked, "Fight? That's ten pops and possible suspension from this week's game."

Jim actually seemed a little scared, which was unusual for him. "You can't do that."

Davis reached for Jim. "Oh Mr. Brown, I can. And I will."

Before Principal Davis could do anything, Lance interceded. "You're wrong, sir. See, I'm new here and I guess I'm a little nervous. Got sick to my stomach, dropped my books, and fell down. Jim here was helping me up." A mischievous grin flashed back at Jim. "Right Jim?"

Jim glared at Lance, still angry, but understood Lance was about to save him. He turned back to the principal. "That's right, Mr. Davis."

The same wicked grin still filled Lance's face when he turned to the jocks, locked eyes with a few, then turned back to Principal Davis. "These guys were just about to pick up my books for me."

A mad scramble ensued as all the players charged to pick up Lance's books, and soon he had them all tucked neatly under his arm.

Lance grinned at the players. "Thanks guys, I really appreciate *everything* you've done for me."

Principal Davis stared down Jim and the jocks. "Back to class."

The jocks scattered and only Principal Davis and Lance remained behind.

The Principal wasn't born yesterday. He had seen similar situations countless times and knew something had actually happened. "Just so you understand, Mr. Renfro, I don't believe you. We don't want trouble makers here."

"Yes, sir."

As Davis walked away Lance grimaced and rubbed his stomach.

***

When Lance entered his next class it was nearly full. As he took his permit to the teacher he noticed the room was divided. The first person he saw was Jim on one side of the class with Cotton, Mike, Marvin and Will. On the other side of the room were Dawn, Sue and Marilyn. The room turned silent. Jim and Dawn glanced at each other. Each of their groups whispered rapidly to each other while Lance faced the teacher.

She read the permit and said, "Welcome to our class, Mr. Renfro. Please find a seat and we'll start the course."

There were only a few empty seats. One was near Jim and one next to Dawn. Lance looked at Dawn and the seat next to her. He turned to Jim who shook his head "No," and slid a finger across his throat. Dawn saw Jim's beheading gesture. When Lance turned back to her she also shook her head no. It wasn't that she didn't want Lance to be near her, but rather feared reprisal from Jim. Lance grinned back at Jim as he moved deliberately to the seat next to Dawn.

Lance said, "Hi again."

"Hi." Dawn leaned slightly toward Lance, and whispered, "Jim is going to freak out."

He whispered back, "I know, he already gave me an encore performance."

Chapter 7

THE CHALLENGE

The male students from the last physical education class of the day ran up the football field to rest a moment, then ran back down the field only to repeat it again. All were exhausted except for a few of the athletic types. Brent, Walter and Lance ran with ease at mid-pack while the jocks Will, Ron and Marvin were way out front.

Coach Turner continued to time them with his stopwatch. He yelled, "Pick it up! The girls run faster than you do."

Across the field Jim led the jocks through football practice. Not far away were Dawn, Joyce Ann, Denise and Sue who practiced their cheer routines for the upcoming game.

Coach Turner walked out on the field and blew his whistle. He seemed disgusted, but that was part of the daily ritual. "Stop! Stop! Listen up!" he announced.

The students gathered around Turner. "Here's what we're going to do. We run again, but this time the top three get to go in."

The students let out with a collective groan. Across the field the jocks and cheerleaders heard the groans and stopped to observe the race. They knew the ritual and they knew what was about to happen, but they enjoyed watching, regardless.

Brent kicked at the dirt and shook his head. "Here we go again."

Coach Turner continued, "The rest will stay out here and continue running until class is over."

Lance shrugged to Walter and Brent. "Hey, you're both good athletes. You can make it."

Walter was upset and already appeared defeated. "Oh we do okay," he said. Then he pointed, "But Ron, Will and Marvin always beat us."

Brent rolled his eyes. "That's why Coach Turner lets the first three go in every day. Those three go to football practice while we keep running back and forth."

Lance had no intention of competing in the race. He could have cared less who won the meaningless competition. He would stay with his friends.

Coach Turner said, "Come on boys and girls, have a little faith. The Good Book says to run by faith and not by sight."

Instantly Lance perked up and was all ears. The Coach had Lance's undivided attention. So it was "faith" again, and he could faintly hear his old minister Barcus Moore. The anger returned and he mumbled, "It's 'walk by faith,' not run, you jerk."

Walter turned to Lance, "What?"

"Nothing."

"Faith won't beat those three," Brent said.

Lance flashed a bit of the rebel anger. "So that's how it is... faith, huh? Well, let's change that today."

This time Brent laughed. "Good luck. They're the fastest guys in school. Maybe the state."

The muscles in Lance's body tensed. He was ready to run now. "Faith won't get me to the finish line, but sight will," he said to Walter and Brent.

Confused, Walter said, "What?"

Lance gritted his teeth, "How about we chunk the faith and live by sight today?"

A slight distance away Coach Turner said, "Remember, the top three."

Walter and Brent were confused, so Lance instantly responded, "Just watch."

Coach Turner yelled, "Ready. Go!"

Instantly, four boys broke into the lead; Ron, Will, Marvin—and Lance! Ron and Will ran like they had been shot out of cannons, but on their heels were Lance and Marvin. At 50 yards it was a four man race, but Marvin appeared slightly slower. Not far behind him, but out of contention, were Brent and Walter along with a half dozen others.

At 80 yards it was Ron, Will and Lance neck-and-neck. This day Marvin would not be third.

Lance took a quick check over his shoulder, saw Marvin, pulled up slightly, and dropped farther behind Ron and Will. However he easily beat Marvin to the finish line.

Ron and Will were stunned to see somebody behind them who wasn't Marvin. The two weren't as amazed as Marvin, Brent, Walter, Dawn, Jim and the rest of the jocks. Nobody had ever crossed the finish line in front of Marvin except Ron and Will.

Mike McClain said to Jim, "Man, that new guy is fast."

Joyce Ann mumbled, "Someone beat Marvin."

Dawn showed a little bit too much excitement. "That's Lance Renfro!" The other cheerleaders failed to notice.

Everyone was amazed. The student runners were still bent over trying to catch their breath. Regardless of their exhaustion they all had smiles and most had turned their eyes on Lance. They now considered him to be one of their own. This was a huge victory for the students. Something they had always dreamed of had finally come to fruition. Ron, Will, Lance and Marvin were clustered together.

Marvin turned to Lance. "Man, you're fast."

Lance managed a grunt and smiled. "I run a lot."

Ron Graham shook his head. "Yeah, and it shows."

The three athletes chuckled and nodded their acceptance to Lance. He had just gained three friends.

Marvin returned to the group of students while Ron, Will and Lance trotted toward the gym.

Coach Turner stared at his stopwatch in disbelief. He watched the three victorious runners and abruptly pursued the boys… but it was Lance he wanted to question.

Lance turned and waved back to Brent and Walter. Their faces were filled with enormous grins as they returned a thumbs-up.

One of the students saw this exchange and tapped Walter on the shoulder. "Who is that guy?"

Walter grinned. "Lance Renfro."

Brent bragged, "He's a friend of ours."

By this time, Coach Turner had almost caught the three victors. He yelled, "Renfro!"

All three stopped and turned around, but Turner waved Ron and Will ahead.

"Yes, sir?"

"If you can play football the way you run, we could use you."

"I don't do organized sports."

"That's too bad because the three of you almost broke the state record."

Lance shrugged. He could have cared less. This was not lost on Turner who had noticed the attitude when Lance coasted into third.

"Why did you let up? Could you have beaten them?"

Lance managed a self-satisfied smirk aimed directly at the coach as though to say, "Wouldn't you like to know." He shrugged again and walked away.

Turner wanted to know. He was curious and determined to find out more about this new loner student.

***

After class Coach Turner walked into the main office and went directly to attendance. He asked if he could take the file of a new student then returned to his office in the gym. He poured a cup of coffee, sat down at his desk and flipped through the student file. The name Lance Renfro was typed on a white sticker and mounted at the top of the manila folder. Turner studied the paperwork. He ran his finger down the sheet of information.

Lance had been a straight "A" student until three years earlier. Overnight he made the transitions to "D's" and "F's," barely managing to pass. Sometimes the last grade would come up and enable him to slide by.

Lance was walking a thin line as far as graduation was concerned. Coach Turner continued through the information until he came to the names of his teachers. Turner stopped on Lance's last coach. He picked up the phone and dialed.

"Coach Clements?"

On the other end Coach Clements responded, "This is Coach Clements. How can I help you?"

"This is Coach Turner in Houston. I'd like to talk to you about a former student, Lance Renfro."

"Lance?" Clements grunted in disgust. "Good luck, you'll need it."

"A troublemaker?"

"No, no, not at all. Just a gifted athlete who's throwing it all away."

"I clocked him in the hundred. Almost a state record."

Clements was stunned and almost rendered speechless, but through his astonishment managed, "How'd you get Lance to run? I never could."

"Top three got out of class."

Clements chuckled before he responded, "That's Renfro, all right." There was a pause. "Have you seen him play football?"

"No."

"If you ever do you're in for a real treat. Honestly, you probably never will."

"Why?"

"He hates organized sports with a passion." Clements' mind reflected on the past and what had happened to Lance. He took a deep breath and sighed. "And maybe for good reason." His tone reflected a little anger. "Give up, Turner. Renfro has some big problems."

"No problem is that big."

"His are. I don't think anyone can save Lance. I really believe he has some type of death wish. I'm sure he still carries that knife."

This could be a real problem, thought Turner, "He fights with a knife?"

"Oh, no, no, not Lance. He's a straight up guy. I'm worried about what he'll do with that knife. It's a major part of his problems."

"Problems?"

For a moment Coach Clements contemplated the future Lance was throwing away. "I'm sorry. I've been trying for three years to help him and to no avail." Clements took a deep breath. "Yeah, it was about three years ago. That's when it happened. It was terrible. It was football season, when.... "

Chapter 8

SANDLOT WARS

After school Brent followed Lance to drop off his Honda. Lance jumped in Brent's van and the boys continued to the sandlot for a little football. Brent drove north on Chimney Rock and turned toward town as he reached Westheimer. They had only gone a couple miles when they reached Yorktown and proceeded north.

To the right was the expensive subdivision of Tanglewood. To the left was a well-manicured park. It was beautiful. A few boys from Lamar were already on the field when Brent pulled up in his van. He, Walter and Lance piled out. Lance's mouth dropped open when he saw the "sandlot." It was everything but a sandlot.

More than a hundred yards from the street was a mansion of enormous proportions. A horseshoe-shaped road led to the front of the estate, longer than two football fields with three hundred feet in width. The mansion was on a prime piece of real estate that stretched almost the length of Yorktown—from Westheimer to San Felipe. The property was a half-mile wide and stretched about a mile in length. The field in which they were about to play "sandlot" football was one of the most pristine parks in all of Houston.

Words couldn't describe the field, but Lance managed, "Awesome!" He bent down and touched the finely manicured grass, comparable to putting greens on a golf course.

"Really something, isn't it?" observed Brent.

Lance shook his head. "They're going to kick us off."

"Not really," said Walter.

Six boys marked the field and prepared to play a little football. As they walked toward the others, Walter continued, "The grounds keeper doesn't mind unless the owner is there, and he usually parks his limo in front."

Lance studied the drive up to the mansion and saw no cars. "Who's the owner?"

"Judge Roy Hofheinz," said Brent.

"The guy who built the Astrodome?"

"Yeah."

"He stays at the Astrodome in a presidential suite," said Walter. "They say it's fancier than this mansion."

Again, Lance marveled at the mansion. "That's hard to believe." He turned back to Brent. "Where are Pug and Steve?"

"Pug's taking care of his foot, but he really doesn't come with us very often. Steve runs track and won't play football," Walter said.

"Too bad."

While they talked a boy arrived on a bike just as another car pulled up. Two boys got out of the car and one of them waved at Brent.

He waved back. "There's Billy Gibbons."

Lance looked him over and nodded. Billy resembled a surfer more than a football player, which was fine with Lance.

"Billy's formed a band and he's pretty good," said Walter. "They call themselves the Moving Sidewalks."

"Yeah, they're good," said Brent. "They play locally at the Catacombs and La Maison."

"We'll take you to hear the band sometime," said Walter.

"Cool," said Lance.

Billy walked up and asked, "Are they coming?"

"I hope not," said Brent.

Lance was about to ask who they meant, but his thoughts were interrupted as Brent introduced him to Billy who was a year younger.

The boys gathered and divided into teams, five from Lamar and five from Lee.

Lance, Brent and Walter brought their team to the imaginary line of scrimmage. The other team was much bigger in physical size. Lance appeared to be an average player. At the same time, it was obvious he wasn't playing to his full ability. He made a tackle. He was tackled. He intercepted the ball and ran it in for a touchdown. The day was just a carefree afternoon of sandlot football.

Again Brent's team huddled. For some reason, Brent and Walter were excited.

Walter said, "Man, we never beat those guys before."

Lance chuckled. "Maybe your luck's about to change."

The game continued as Lance and his new friends maintained their lead over the Lamar boys.

A red '67 Corvette pulled up and stopped. The ten sandlot players halted their game and watched as more cars pulled up.

One of the sandlot players from Lamar grunted. He was almost angry. "They're here."

Jim got out of his Corvette. The jocks had arrived. Players from the Lee football team rolled out of their cars and strutted toward Lance and the other sandlot players.

Irritated, Brent turned to Lance. "Time to beat it."

Lance was more than irritated. He was angry. "No. They can leave."

Walter's jaw dropped. "Are you crazy?"

Fifteen jocks rolled as a unit toward the ten players. Surrounding Jim like an immovable force were Mike, Bill, Cotton, Will, Marvin and Ron. Lance had run against a few of the boys at school and therefore knew of their athletic ability.

Jim sneered at the sandlot players. "Beat it. This is our place."

Some of the jocks laughed. Hands clenched to fists, Lance didn't move. A surge of anger overwhelmed him—a metamorphosis that changed him into a completely different person. He wrestled internally for control as most of others walked away. Nobody had even noticed the change in Lance.

"No!" said Lance. "We were here first. You can leave."

Stunned, the boys who were walking away stopped and turned around to observe the confrontation. A mixture of curiosity and shock not only kept the boys there, but also lured them back toward Lance. There was still time to run if needed, but at that moment, something changed in them all.

"We can kick your ass," said Bill Martin.

Lance's quick wit emerged as he engaged in verbal battle. "I'm sure *all* of you can. I doubt *you* can."

The jocks moved forward. The sandlot players behind Lance hesitated and gasped. A couple of them backed a few feet away in slight fear of what might happen next.

Jim menaced, "How about I feed you a fist sandwich?"

Lance refused to give ground. "Not hungry."

A few of the jocks, along with Cotton, Marvin, Will and Mike chuckled. Jim's temper got the best of him and he moved toward Lance, chomping at the bit for a physical confrontation. Cotton and Bill restrained him.

"Get outta here!" Jim threatened again.

With one finger outstretched, Lance took time to count the jocks.

While he counted the halt in action Brent regained a long lost confidence. "We used to play together in elementary," he reminded the jocks.

Jim grunted and Mike said, "That was a long time ago."

Jim smirked and mocked, "You're Has Beens. Yesterday's Heroes." Confused, he watched as Lance kept counting something with his fingers. "What are you doing?"

With a smile of confidence Lance finished counting and said, "Let's see, I count about fifteen. We have ten. That'll give you the extras you'll need to play against us."

The sandlot players chuckled as Brent and Walter moved to each side of Lance. The other seven also clustered around him. For the first time ever, these boys had stood their ground. It felt good.

Stunned, Jim blurted, "The *what?*"

Lance stepped forward. That day nine others took the step of defiance with him.

Lance said, "Extras you'll need if you play us."

Brent whispered to Lance, "Are you crazy?"

Bill Martin said, "No way we're gonna play you."

It appeared nothing would stop Lance. "So all of you are chicken?"

A couple of those gathered around Lance gasped as Jim charged with the intent of extracting revenge. This time it took Mike, Will and Cotton to restrain him. Lance stood his ground.

Lance continued, "First one to get three touchdowns ahead wins. Three complete passes is a first down."

Jim calmed down and exuded confidence. This boded ill for the sandlot players. "Okay. We'll play you. You can even have the ball first."

The jocks all laughed. They knew this challenge would be over swiftly. The inexperienced players before them were easy pickings.

None were more astonished than the sandlot players who had always been run off the field. Today they would stay and play against overwhelming odds.

Both sides formed huddles and Lance gave the football to Brent. "Okay Brent, call the play."

One of the players said to Lance, "You're gonna get us killed."

Lance grinned. "Isn't it great!"

Most of the players in the huddle chuckled and shook their heads in disbelief.

Brent spun the football in his hand. "We can't beat them."

Lance's confidence never wavered. "I never said we could, but we can do better than you think."

Brent said, "We can't keep up with Ron and Will. Jim's gonna kill us with TD passes."

"Today will surprise all of you," encouraged Lance. "Today you'll stand up and not back down."

"Yeah, but I still want to be able to play my guitar this weekend," said Billy as he peered at his fingers.

The other nine listened, catching the esprit de corps. Before Lance's eyes he witnessed the sandlot players metamorphose into a cohesive unit.

Jim lined up the jocks. The sandlot players came to the line.

Brent called the signals. Curtis Sanford played free safety for the jocks and didn't appear quite ready for action. This was something Lance noticed before the first play—Curtis lacked something. It appeared it might just simply be skill.

The jocks sacked Brent on the first play.

In the huddle Lance took control. "We need quick plays. Everybody run up five and come back for the ball. Brent, hit the one's who are open. Those jocks won't be able to defend against the quick plays."

On the next play Brent connected for a gain of about ten yards. For the first time ever, the students moved with a building confidence.

For the next play Lance ran down the line of scrimmage, took the pass from Brent, and scooted in and around the jocks until he was tackled from behind after a huge gain.

Near the sidelines a '66 Chevy Impala pulled up. Out danced Dawn, Joyce Ann, Marilyn, Denise and Sue. They carried an ice chest filled with glass bottles of Cokes and other assorted drinks to the sidelines to watch the game. Sue took out a "church key," popped the top on one of the bottles and chugged the drink. All of the girls were surprised to see Jim and the jocks playing a game against the sandlot players. This was a first.

Brent kept gazing at Joyce Ann. When she stared back he lost all composure. Walter and Lance laughed and reminded him he was playing football. On the very next play, Brent threw an interception.

Dawn waved and shouted, "Jim!"

Jim nodded in frustration as though he was too busy. He ignored her, which hurt her feelings—until she noticed Lance.

In the jock huddle Jim barked commands. "Ron, streak down the left and I'll hit you for the score. Let's get this over with."

They all wore smug grins as they came to the line. Lance set himself as the free safety. Walter and Brent noticed his intensity and focus, although the jocks did not. To them, Lance was just another sandlot player.

Confident, Jim rolled back. The blocking was excellent. None of the sandlot players could get through. Jim lofted a perfect spiral. Ron reached for the ball—it looked like a sure touchdown! Out of nowhere Lance came across at the last second and knocked the ball away.

The students were stunned and excited all at the same time.

Cotton gawked at the play downfield. "Wow! Did you see that?"

Jim growled, "Shut-up. Huddle."

As they returned to their huddles Lance peered at Dawn. When their eyes met he grinned and waved. She waved back but unexpectedly felt guilty and checked to make sure Jim didn't see.

Brent gazed at the cheerleaders and caught Joyce Ann appearing to wave. *At him?* Mechanically he glanced backwards. Surely somebody was standing behind him, for no cheerleader, especially Joyce Ann, would ever wave at a guy like him. But to his astonishment nobody was around and it felt like an electrical shock. Brent Baughman just got noticed by a cheerleader. Nothing like this had ever happened to him. Somehow he managed to smile and wave back. Joyce Ann jumped up and down and returned the smile and waved again.

Excited, Brent ran to Lance and Walter. "Man, you won't believe this... but Joyce Ann waved at me!"

Walter didn't believe him. "I don't think so. Not Joyce Ann. She's the prettiest girl in school."

Lance frowned at the others. "Why not? Maybe she likes you."

Unable to grasp the possibility Brent responded, "Me? But she's a cheerleader!"

"So?" Lance pointed at the jocks and took a moment to lock eyes with each of the sandlot players. "We're playing them straight up and doing well. You can do whatever you want, and that includes Joyce Ann." He flashed a wicked smile. "Plus, you have something none of them have… " He paused to build their curiosity. "Brains."

When the sandlot broke out in hysterical laughter all other eyes turned to them. Even the cheerleaders wondered what was so funny.

The laughing irritated the jocks and an irate spirit continued to build within Jim. "They think it's funny? They won't be laughing after the next play."

"Who do they think they are?" demanded Mike.

"That dork should be exhausted by now. Okay Will, down the right and burn him."

Will flashed a wicked smile as they came to the line.

The cheerleaders yelled encouragement. Luckily no one saw Dawn and Joyce Ann gazing at Lance and Brent.

Jim took the snap and Will streaked down the sideline, but yet again Lance managed to deflect the pass.

The jocks huddled rapidly.

Ron Graham said, "He's good."

Will Coleman added, "Yeah, and fast."

The admiration in their voices wasn't lost on Jim, "Ron and Will, quick slant. I'll hit the open guy."

They came to the line. Jim took the snap and threw a quick slant which Ron snatched in full-stride. But before he could turn up field Lance tackled him.

With each huddle Jim became angrier. "Cotton, up the middle and take out that dork!"

Cotton smirked. He took the hand-off and charged ahead. He smacked Lance who still managed to pop back up after the tackle.

"Our ball," Lance announced, grinning.

Jim's mouth dropped open. "What?" He shook his head. "No way!"

Cotton confirmed, "We didn't make it Jim. Remember, three complete passes is a first. You only had one."

Jim was stunned. This had never happened to him.

Something else happened that Lance had not intended. He had taken over. He was the leader and all heads, including Brent's, now turned to him for the next play.

Lance said, "Who is their safety?"

Walter snickered, "Curtis Sanford."

Billy Gibbons said, "Curtis is the reason we lost state last year."

Brent agreed, "Probably the only reason we might not win this year, either."

Lance smiled. "Good. He didn't look too sharp. Listen Brent, when you take the snap count to five then throw the ball at Curtis like he's the receiver."

Brent furrowed his brow. "I thought we wanted to win?"

Lance nodded. "Trust me. I wanna see something."

Brent took the snap and his lips moved to the numbers. The jocks charged him hard. Lance ran up the side and cut toward Curtis. Brent fired the ball just as he was hit with amazing force from the football team. When Curtis saw the ball spiral toward him, he was traumatized and did a nervous jitterbug. The poor jock looked more like an eager puppy ready to pee on the floor than a football player. He braced for the catch, but at the last instant Lance cut in front of him, took the ball and raced into the end zone untouched!

A collective groan came from the jocks, but the cheers of the opposing nine players drowned out their whimpers. With that play the sandlot players took the lead!

Dawn cheered momentarily, but glares from the other cheerleaders and Jim silenced her.

Joyce Ann was free-spirited. "Wow! Did you see that touchdown pass?"

Lance walked toward Jim and tossed him the ball as he continued to his team. "Your ball, hot-shot."

Again, the jocks were forced to restrain Jim.

After Cotton released him, Jim glared intently at Lance, shook his head and mumbled, "Man, that guy has a death wish."

From the sidelines Joyce Ann whispered in Dawn's ear, "He's nifty."

"Who?"

Joyce Ann pointed. "Brent."

Dawn was flabbergasted, "Joyce Ann! What about our guys?"

Joyce Ann was a little defensive. "Then why did you cheer for Lance?"

Dawn waved Joyce Ann off, but when she turned back to the game she took a long hard look at Lance and actually wondered why she cheered for him. She always knew what she wanted. Now suddenly she was confused.

In Lance's huddle Billy said, "My God, we have the lead!"

Brent and Walter looked at each other, stunned. Their eyes turned to the reason they were ahead. All in the huddle looked to Lance for instructions. He failed to notice because he was completely focused on the game.

The jocks came to the line. Jim took the snap, dropped back and fired a perfect spiral far down field. The players backed off to gape at what appeared to be a sure touchdown. Ron went up for the pass, but Lance clung to him like a shadow stride-for-stride. Lance tipped the ball, but as they came down this time Lance managed to juggle the ball and work it toward him, then clutched it firmly before smashing to the ground.

Lance jumped up with the ball and started to make a huddle, but looked up to see everyone perfectly still. It was reminiscent of a freeze frame photo.

The same words erupted from the mouths of everyone: "Interception!"

In amazement Cotton said, "I can't believe I just saw that."

Stunned, Dawn mumbled, "Lance intercepted!"

Lance's teammates ran to the huddle. Some patted him on the back while everyone stared at him, awestruck.

Lance pulled back and stood up straight. "Okay, what's wrong with everybody?"

Brent's jaw hung wide open, resembling someone who had just seen a spectacular historical event. "You intercepted Jim Brown."

Lance laughed. "Yeah, that's what it's called. So?"

Walter explained, "No one has ever intercepted Brown."

Lance snickered, "Well, someone has now."

Another player remarked, "He was never intercepted last year."

Billy shrugged. "Or the year before. I don't really like him, but Brown's the best in state."

Things were totally different in the jock huddle. Jim berated Curtis and pushed him. Mike and Cotton had to pull him away. But they couldn't keep Jim from getting in Curtis' face. "If you played football the way he does, we'd have won state last year."

The jocks were angry and played to more than their full potential on the next play. They managed to intercept Brent's pass.

In the jock huddle, Jim made plans and it didn't bode well for one particular person. "Marvin wide. Cotton up the middle."

Marvin stood erect. "I'm a running back."

Jim smiled at Marvin. "I know. Pick Renfro."

Cotton charged up the middle. Lance moved to meet him, but Marvin blind-sided him with a vicious hit. Lance went down and groaned in pain. Cotton finished his run for the touchdown.

Of all the cheerleaders, only Dawn showed concern. Suspicious, Marilyn scrutinized her.

Lance gasped for air. Marvin stepped over to Lance, straddled him, reached down and pulled Lance up by his pants. "Suck air man. Suck air," Marvin encouraged.

Jim marched to the sidelines. "His game's over."

Cotton went over to help Marvin. Lance crawled to his knees and tried to shake off the hit.

Cotton put a hand on Lance's shoulder. "You okay?"

Lance nodded and tried to stand. He wobbled a little, then grinned slightly at Cotton, "Did you score?"

Cotton nodded.

Lance yelled, "Huddle up, our ball."

Cotton and Marvin shook their heads in disbelief and walked back to their side.

"He's one tuff dude," Cotton mumbled.

Marvin shook his head. "I was afraid I hurt him."

Both had gained a new respect for this tuff little player.

With the touchdown, the jocks regained some of their confidence. Jim played rough, taking time to stiff-arm the opposing team players whenever possible. He tried to aim for the throat. But he still had a difficult time connecting with his passes and each missed pass made him angrier. On one play, he stiff-armed the tackler, Walter, in the neck. Walter fell to the ground, chocked and gasped for air. The players rushed to his aid and after a moment he was better—although, he still had a hard time speaking. No one was angrier than Lance. He wanted revenge and he got it on the very next play.

When Jim took the snap it was obvious he was going to run, and this was what Lance anticipated. Lance took the opportunity to charge toward Jim. When Jim saw Lance advance toward him, it was just what he wanted. He stiffened his arm with the intention of jamming his arm down Lance's throat. Jim was inches away from hitting him when Lance suddenly dropped and hit Jim below the knees. The hit made Jim do a complete somersault before he smashed into the ground.

Jim yelled, "I'm gonna break you in half!" He jumped up and charged Lance with the intention of beating him to a pulp.

Lance stood his ground ready to fight back, but Cotton, Ron, and Marvin pulled Jim back.

Still Jim yelled, "You do that again and I'm going to kick your ass!"

Those who played with Jim and against him knew that when he said it, he was serious.

But Lance didn't care. Under control but still angry, he yelled back, "You stick that hand in my face again and I'm going to bite your fingers off!" He turned and walked back to the huddle.

Cotton kept pulling Jim back and looked back at Lance. "He's crazy."

When Lance got back to the huddle Brent had his hands in his pocket and whistled as though he was up to no good.

Lance noticed, frowned and asked, "What's wrong with you?"

"Nothing." Brent smirked, "I'm not going to stick my fingers in your face."

Everyone in the huddle chuckled, even Lance.

The jocks scored when Cotton ran in for another touchdown. Even though they fell behind, the sandlot players managed to stay up with Brown and Lee's football team.

In the huddle Lance grinned at Brent. "At the snap, the End pushed hard and caught the defense off guard."

"What?" Brent was taken back at the words, which were a line from his poem.

"Hey Brent, you ready to catch that touchdown pass?" asked Lance. Brent shrugged and Lance continued. "I'll line up behind you on the right. Pitch back to me then run straight up field. It'll be a lateral." He smiled. "Brent, you're about to catch a touchdown pass over Curtis."

All the players chuckled. The play went to perfection as Lance started to run forward, then seemed to retreat. When the players charged him, he lofted a perfect spiral downfield over the unsuspecting Curtis Sanford. Brent gave it all he could, but it appeared the pass was too long. Somehow he managed to get a few fingers on the ball and finally hauled it in for a touchdown. The sandlot team went crazy, but everybody else was silent—except for Joyce Ann, who also cheered Brent's touchdown.

Lance and Walter ran to congratulate Brent on his touchdown against Robert E. Lee's finest. Jim and the others felt the sandlot players celebrated a little too long. Jim huddled his team and the game started again.

The jocks were ahead, but only by a touchdown. Lance was the major reason they couldn't put it away. Each time the jocks scored, the sandlot players managed to respond with a touchdown of their own. Brent had passed for two more touchdowns, which was more than Jim Brown! With each passing play the players on Lance's team gained more confidence and reflected their newfound assurance. Although most felt it was all because of Lance, they were playing like winners. The sandlot team played above their ability while the jocks were now playing below their normal level.

In the jock huddle Jim had become unhinged—worse than jocks had never seen. It affected his playing and his teammates. Still, Jim's anger didn't even come close to the way he felt. His face was livid and red. Slobber actually spewed from his mouth as he yelled, "We should be way ahead of those dorks!"

Bill Martin said, "Face it, those dorks are giving us a run for our money."

With half a grin of amazement Cotton mumbled, "One guy is beating us."

"Yeah, that's what makes it worse," snickered Will.

Jim shook his fists in the air. "I want him out."

Ron Graham didn't like the tone. "Leave him alone, we're ahead."

Jim would not be denied. He wanted revenge. His face lit up with an evil smile. "Ron, Will, slant. The ball's coming to our friend—sandwich him!"

Ron and Will were reluctant but lined up for the play.

Jim dropped back, waited and fired the football up the middle. When Lance touched the ball he was smashed below the knees and at the shoulders. He did one and a half flips, coming down hard on his shoulders and neck. The severe jolt appeared bad, as if he had broken multiple bones. He didn't move.

Most of the players stared in disbelief. Jim walked away only to see Marilyn, Joyce Ann and Dawn run toward Lance. Jim grabbed Dawn.

"Where do you think you're going?"

Dawn jerked away. "He could be hurt."

Lance's teammates rushed to his side along with Ron, Will, Marvin and Cotton. When they reached Lance, he still clutched the football in his arm.

The awe in Brent's voice said it all: "Another interception!"

Even Cotton was amazed. "Look! He's still holding the ball!"

As they stared at Lance he managed to hold the ball up, wave it and mumble, "Our ball."

All the players laughed and let out a sigh of relief. Then Lance dropped the ball and appeared to pass out.

Dawn slid to her knees next to Lance. She took his hand and rubbed his forehead. Marilyn moved next to Cotton.

Joyce Ann rubbed up against Brent, touched his arm and asked, "Brent, is he okay?"

The contact excited Brent. He never expected Joyce Ann to be at his side, much less touch him. For a fleeting moment Lance was forgotten. Brent was tongue-tied. He had always dreamed of Joyce Ann, but in those dreams he knew what to say. He had every word down perfect. But now his mind was empty. He looked her in the eyes and finally managed, "I think so."

With a slight smile she took his arm with her hands. "That touchdown you threw was neato."

"Really?"

She nodded back to him and squeezed his arm.

"Thanks."

All of the sandlot players circled Lance, which also included most of the jocks.

"You okay, man?" Will asked.

Cotton touched Dawn on the shoulder and she glanced back at him. "Is he okay?" he asked, worried.

She shrugged and turned back to Lance. "Lance, Lance, are you okay?"

Will and Ron were on their knees next to him.

Lance's eyes fluttered open and he gave the appearance of being drunk and lost. He saw Dawn and beamed. "Oh, wow. I must be in heaven. I see an angel." He reached up and touched her face gently.

"Aw, how sweet," said Marilyn.

Many laughed. They were all relieved.

Cotton said, "He's delirious."

Brent shook his head. "He's talking from his heart." He peeked back at Joyce Ann and she squeezed his arm.

Lance blinked rapidly and appeared confused. "What am I doing here?"

Relieved, Dawn grunted, "Football. Remember?"

Things were coming back to him, but he was still a little groggy. "Football?"

Recognition came slowly. A moment later he managed a smile and pointed to Ron and Will. "Oh yeah, you two tried to kill me."

Both boys cringed. Ron said, "We didn't mean to hurt you."

Will was also rapid to respond, "You are one tuff player."

Lance took a deep breath and let it out, "I'm not that tuff. I'm finished for the day." He smiled at Dawn and squeezed her hand. "If it's okay, I think I'll lay here for a little bit longer."

Everyone laughed as the crowd started to disperse.

Chapter 9

SLUMBER PARTY

All the cheerleaders had gathered at Dawn's house for a sleepover. Marilyn was also there. The girls were in their pajamas and formed a circle on the floor to discuss the upcoming game along with other cheerleading items. Music from a small record player and a stack of vinyl 45's filled the room. The needle gave off a slight crackle as the Chiffons sung the joyful melody *One Fine Day.*

They talked about the football game and started humming and singing to the tune.

"Brent is so fine," said Joyce Ann.

Sue King rolled her lips back in a sneer. "Brent Baughman? He's groady."

The comment made Joyce Ann angry. "Is not."

"Is too."

Joyce Ann stuck her nose up and turned away from Sue, "He's neato."

Denise Collins was almost in shock. "Joyce Ann, you're not going out with him... are you?"

Joyce Ann hesitated and wondered why she felt the way she did about Brent. She considered the facts: Brent was sweet and not like the volatile jocks. He never appeared to be angry. And he was cute. That was enough for her. Defiantly, she held her head up and smiled. "Maybe."

Again Denise was taken back at this revelation. "He doesn't even play football."

"He looked pretty good to me, Denise," said Joyce Ann.

Sue was angry. "How can you do that to us?"

Joyce Ann snickered. "Me? What about Dawn? She was making goo goo eyes at Lance!"

All the girls whipped their heads around to Dawn. A new record dropped down and the Toys led in with *Lover's Concerto.*

Dawn was defensive. "I wasn't making goo goo eyes at anybody. I was uh, just uh, admiring his interception."

Now Sue was suspicious. "Joyce Ann's right. You were cheering when Lance made the touchdown."

"It seems you enjoyed holding his hand and rubbing his head just a little too much," added Denise

"He was hurt."

"How could you do that to Jim?" accused Sue.

"I didn't do anything to Jim."

The three girls frowned and rolled their eyes.

Sue waved a finger at her. "Dawn, you're making a big mistake. Lance Renfro is an outsider. Everyone envies the fact you're with Jim."

They all turned and looked at Dawn, as though they agreed with Sue. Sue fantasized about Jim as she held her hands to her chest. "If Jim were mine I'd do anything for him."

Joyce Ann grunted and swung her pillow, hitting Sue in the face.

Sue gasped and all the girls laughed, even Sue.

***

The three boys lounged on the bank of Buffalo Bayou, near the rope. Walter and Lance waited for Brent to swing across.

In deep thought as though he had remembered something, Brent turned to Lance. "What happened to you today?"

Lance shrugged and took a swig of his beer. "I got pounded."

The answer had nothing to do with what Brent wanted to know. He was referring to the radical change in Lance during the game. "No. I mean the way you played. It was like you were Doctor Jekyll with us and Mr. Hyde when Jim and the others arrived. Man, you were really wicked against them."

Lance cringed as though he was pushed into a corner. "I just don't like guys like them; the way they bully the weak. There is no reason to be a bully and treat people the way they do."

"Well, they sure didn't bully you. I thought you had a death wish."

With a grin of satisfaction, Walter commented, "Mr. Hyde was awesome."

Brent asked, "You ever think about playing--."

Lance interrupted loudly, "No! I don't do team sports."

From his tone and actions it was obvious he was angry. His tirade came as somewhat of a surprise and Brent and Walter looked at each other, slightly concerned.

Brent held his hands up defensively. "Hey, no problem. Sorry I asked."

Instantly Lance mellowed, "No, I'm sorry."

Confused, Brent shook his head, "It's just that you're really good. If I was half what you are I'd be on our football team."

"Thanks, but I won't play. I have my reasons."

"Hey, not my problem," said Brent. He arched his back, ran a few steps, and swung out over the bayou.

Chapter 10
COACH TURNER FORCES A CHALLENGE

Coach Turner blew his whistle to signal the end of practice. He motioned his players to gather around. Every day after practice and before and after every game, he had them say a prayer. The players went to one knee and bowed their heads. Turner intoned, "Lord, we want to thank you for another safe practice. Let your spirit be with us and please heal Skip; we need him back. Thank you Lord, Amen."

In unison the players said, "Amen."

"Hold up!" said Turner. "Before the showers I want a few players to remain on the field with me." His tone had a slight edge of anger and they noticed it. "All those who played sandlot football the other day remain here. I know who you are, so don't try to sneak in with the others unless you want a good tanning. You know I will. The rest of you hit the showers."

The players cringed. Jim, Curtis, Cotton, Bill, Mike, Ron, Will, Marvin and the others remained behind. They did not want the pops, but from the tone of his voice they already knew Coach Turner was livid.

He paced back and forth for about a minute, then stopped and faced the guilty players. With hands behind his back, he glared at each. "Don't all of you be idiots! There is a reason we don't want you to play sandlot ball. You could get hurt and ruin the season for all of us!"

All were solemn, but Jim smirked. "We weren't the ones who got hurt."

The anger was more intense when Turner rolled his head toward Jim. "Hurting people is not what this game is about, Mr. Brown! Have you forgotten what happened to Skip?"

Jim knew and nodded his head.

Turner continued, "Skip is probably out for the season for doing the same thing. Now we must rely on Curtis to be our free safety." All of the players hung their heads down. Turner hesitated before he asked the burning question, "Brown, I heard you got intercepted?"

"Twice," Ron quipped.

Turner was taken back at Ron's words. He turned his head slowly so he could study Jim. "Twice?"

Jim grunted and shrugged it off. "We were just screwing around. It meant nothing."

"It means something every time you throw that football," snapped Turner. "Do I need to remind you that our first game is in a few days? We can't win if you throw interceptions to a nobody sandlot player!" He paused to let his words sink in and with a disgusted wave of his hand continued, "Everybody to the showers and be ready for a hard practice tomorrow afternoon."

Everyone groaned and walked away.

Coach Turner motioned with his finger. "Ron, Will, Cotton—hold up."

The three boys sighed as their shoulders drooped and they turned back to the coach. After everyone else was gone Turner was relaxed and calm. This put the boys at ease and that is exactly what the coach wanted. He knew he could trust these three players.

"Who were you playing? Guys from Lamar?"

"Some of them," said Ron.

"A Lamar player intercepted Jim?"

"No," said Cotton.

Turner was momentarily stunned. "From here?"

All three nodded yes.

Who could have intercepted Brown? A guy not on the team? The coach's mind couldn't imagine who had managed the feat. "Who on earth intercepted Brown?" he asked.

Will leaned forward. "Remember the guy who beat Marvin?"

"Renfro."

"Yeah, he intercepted both times."

Coach Turner was stunned and he remembered Clements words: *If you ever see him play you're in for a real treat.*

"And he kept up with me, coach," said Ron.

Turner eyed him for a moment, "Renfro is as fast as you?"

Ron nodded, "Yes, sir."

Will snickered, "He also burned Curtis."

The groan from Turner said it all. "Everyone burns Curtis, but he's the best we've got until Skip returns. If he returns."

With a shake of his head Ron said, "Renfro is better than any safety I ever played against. Even Skip."

The surprise was evident in Turner's eyes because he considered Skip the best free safety he had ever seen in his coaching tenure. "Nobody is better than Skip."

"Renfro is!" said Ron.

"Yeah," said Will.

"For sure," said Cotton.

Turner could see the boys were serious and their respect for Renfro was reflected not only in their words, but also in their eyes.

Something came to Will. "No matter where the ball went, Renfro was always there."

The Coach saw the admiration when Cotton said, "Coach, it's like the ball was metal and he was a magnet."

Ron nodded in agreement.

Will, however, shook his head. "Naw, Cotton. Renfro is more like a spider web."

"What do you mean?" Turner asked.

Will shrugged. "Well Coach, you ever walk into a spider web and try to get it off? The more you try to get it off, the more it sticks to you. You just can't get rid of it. Well, that's Renfro, for sure. I couldn't get rid of him."

Ron agreed. "For sure, Coach. Renfro is like a spider web. Once he gets on you, you're not gonna get him off."

"And he's one tuff player, Coach," said Cotton sincerely.

"Yeah," Ron and Will agreed.

The player's obvious respect for Renfro was not lost on Turner, but it was still hard to fathom Brown being intercepted, much less twice and by the same player. Turner furrowed his brows and grunted. "Maybe Brown threw a bad pass?"

In unison all three of the athletes shook their heads and declared, "No."

Cotton continued to shake his head. "No, Coach. I saw the passes to Ron and Will. All were on the money. Renfro just got his hands in there, somehow."

"Yeah, Coach. I've never seen anything like it," Will agreed.

Coach Turner rubbed his lips with his fingers. "Thanks, boys. Get back to your classes."

The boys ran off and Turner returned to the gym.

At his office Turner leaned over his desk and pulled out the folder with the name Lance Renfro. He slapped the folder against his palm and began to form a plan. "Okay Renfro, let's see just how fast you are."

***

The next day Turner grew impatient while waiting to put his plan into motion. The P. E. class continued to run back and forth on the football field and Coach Turner was ready to move into action. He observed the students but he kept his eyes on Lance. The students reached the end of the field and were ready to run again when the coach blew his whistle. The time had come.

Ron, Will, Marvin, Brent, Walter, and Lance remained clustered while they waited for Coach Turner to set up the daily contest. They had become friends after the sandlot game and it was all due to Lance. Some wanted to see if the coach would change the rules and allow four to go in so Marvin could continue with football practice. The students wanted to see Lance beat Marvin again. The jocks and cheerleaders had paused to observe the challenge unfold, whatever it might be.

"Okay we're going to do something different today. Graham, Coleman and Renfro over here," yelled the coach.

The three ran over to Turner.

"A one hundred yard race; losers get ten pops."

Again the students grumbled. Mechanically, Ron and Will moved to their position.

"Quiet," said the coach.

Lance refused to go to the starting line for the new challenge and continued to face Turner, who pointed to Ron and Will.

"Over there, Renfro."

"I know what you're doing, and I'm not going to do it."

"Get over there now or come with me and get pops."

Lance took two steps toward Turner. "Let's get it over with. I'll take the pops."

The students did a collective groan of disbelief. They wanted to see Lance run.

This was not what Turner expected. He was somewhat taken by surprise when Lance defied him, but he could not back down at that point. So he motioned Lance ahead and led him to his office.

Dismayed at the unexpected change in events, Ron, Will, Brent, Walter and the others watched the coach and Lance walk away.

Ron said, "Man, Lance is crazy."

Brent agreed, "Tell me about it. Sometimes I just don't understand him."

"No way I'd take pops from Coach Turner," said Will.

Chapter 11

FRIDAY NIGHT LIGHTS

The bell rang signaling the end of school for the day. What had been a quiet school campus now resembled an ant mound someone had kicked open. In seconds students exited from every opening and emptied the school—a human stampede. They may have been slow in school, but they were fast getting home.

Brent and Walter ran after Lance who had just started his motorcycle. When Lance saw them coming he shut the engine down and climbed off his Honda.

"Why didn't you run?" Brent asked.

Lance shrugged, "I didn't like what Coach Turner was trying to do."

Walter said, "Man, but ten pops from Coach Turner… "

"And with Moses," said Brent

Moses was what Coach Turner called the paddle he used when he gave pops to those who misbehaved, broke the rules or defied him. Moses was drilled with ten holes which the coach dubbed the "Ten Commandments," to keep the students in line. The holes prevented a cushion of air so the pops reached maximum intensity.

The pops appeared to have had no effect on Lance. "Yeah, I met Moses and the Ten Commandments. No big deal. I've had pops before. Lots of them."

Fear was evident when Walter spoke. "I can't take pops. That paddle scares me."

Alarmed at Walter's admission, Lance said, "You're afraid of pops?"

"Yeah. I always cry and the guys laugh at me."

The pops meant nothing to Lance, but the few words Walter mumbled about the pops truly concerned him.

The three agreed to meet later and go to the game together.

***

Students from both sides of Delmar Stadium cheered as the Lee Generals and the Bellaire Cardinals engaged in battle. The game had gotten off to a bad start for Lee when Bellaire scored on a long bomb over Curtis on the first play after the kickoff. Brown and Dickey along with Ron and Will had kept Lee in contention, but near the end of the first half Lee was still down a touchdown in a high scoring game.

In the first row of the stands, near midfield, Lance, Brent, Walter and Marilyn yelled encouragement. The cheerleaders also did their part to lather up the school spirit. Dawn continued to peek casually in Lance's direction which caused her to almost miss a flip.

When Bellaire came to the line Lance jumped to the railing, cupped his hands around his mouth and yelled at the free safety, "Curtis, up left. It's a down and out. Up left! Move up Curtis, move up!"

Turner, Dawn, Cotton, Jim and many others turned and listened. Swiftly, everyone who had heard Lance turned back to watch the play unfold, curious as to whether Lance's prediction was accurate. Bellaire executed a perfect down and out to their right—just like Lance had said!

Coach Turner, Dawn and a few others turned back to look at Lance, amazement evident on their faces. Disgusted, Lance swung his fists in the air and sat back down.

With a furrowed brow Brent asked, "How'd you do that?"

A little confused, Lance said, "Do what?"

"Know what play they were going to run."

Lance shrugged. "I don't really know. I just see it and feel it."

Bellaire broke the huddle and came to the line.

Again Lance saw something, "Oh no, they're going to burn Curtis again." He jumped to his feet, moved to the railing and yelled, "Curtis, back up quick! Deep pass!" Lance waved his arm for Curtis to move back.

Again heads turned to Lance and many turned back to the field to see if he was correct again.

"Back, Curtis! Back, drop back!" Lance yelled.

Bellaire ran the play. They executed a long pass and burned Curtis for another touchdown.

Some of the students and jocks gave Lance a strange look. Some were in awe and some were angry. Lance sat back down on the bleacher and shook his head.

Dawn was amazed. "How'd he know?"

Jim Brown was torqued. "Dork."

Dickey was fascinated. "How can he read the offense like that?"

Turner, on the other hand, was livid and marched toward Lance. He stopped just before the railing. "Renfro!"

Lance stood up and walked to the railing. He too was angry. "Yeah, Coach?"

"If you want to coach the defense, then join the team and come down on the field now!"

"I don't do team sports."

"Good! Then shut up!"

Turner spun around and without even glancing back returned to the team.

Lance yelled at Coach Turner, "Spread the linebackers. Drop the left corner back to help Curtis! Coach?"

Turner never looked back. Lance grunted his disgust and hit the rails with his fist. He returned to his seat next to Brent and Walter. He glared at the opposing team and the bleachers filled with their fans and continued to stare at the other side of the stadium. With a wicked smile Lance locked eyes with Brent and Walter. He grinned and said, "If we're going to win, we need more team spirit. Something big to get us going."

"Like what?" said Brent.

"I don't know yet."

The referee blew his whistle signaling the end of the first half. Both teams trotted off the field.

Lance slowly glanced around, looking for something that would help his newly hatching plan… although he had no idea what it might be. Next to the cheerleaders was the team banner about six feet tall and eight feet wide emblazoned with "ROBERT E. LEE GENERALS." The letters were enormous next to a huge character of the old General. Lance looked across to the stands on the other side. A smile creased his face. Excited, he turned to Walter and Brent with mischief in his eyes.

"You have team spirit?"

Both boys saw his enthusiasm and were a little bit worried.

Walter hesitated but shook his head. "Yeah."

"Wanna have some fun?"

Brent grimaced. "Depends. Will we get suspended?"

Lance laughed out loud. "Probably."

Brent could not remember when he had so much fun in his life since Lance's arrival. Surfside had been a great adventure, and the sandlot football experience was beyond description. He also now had Joyce Ann, or almost had her. What other wild adventures lay ahead with Lance he had no way of knowing, but one thing was for sure—whatever Lance dreamed up would be exciting regardless of the trouble or the problems they encountered.

Brent rolled his lip and nodded his head. "Count me in."

"Oh, no," said Walter. "Guys, I don't like this." Brent and Lance frowned at Walter, who at that moment realized he'd be missing out on the fun. "Oh, okay."

The cheerleaders finished a cheer and Lance signaled to Dawn. She saw him and moved to the railing.

She was curious. "How did you know that player was going deep?"

Lance tried to wave off the question. "It's hard to explain… can you do me a favor?"

"I'll try… "

"I want to borrow the team banner."

Dawn was suspicious but agreed to his request.

***

A few minutes later near the end zone, Lance, Walter and Brent carried the rolled up banner toward the Bellaire side. They took the banner to the edge of the bleachers and climbed the steps to the top of the concrete seating. When they reached the top, the boys continued down the bleachers until they reached midfield. They sat down and waited.

They didn't have long to wait. After only a few minutes in their seats they watched as both teams trotted to their respective sidelines for the beginning of the second half.

At the top of the Bellaire bleachers Walter, Brent and Lance stood up. Lance and Brent climbed on top of the short concrete wall that lined the back of the stadium. Walter handed one end of the banner to Lance then walked over to Brent and gave him the other end of the banner.

Lance signaled to Brent that he was ready. Both held the corners and released the giant banner at the same time, allowing it to roll open.

The Lee counter attack on Lamar came when the stars and bars waved proudly over Redskin stands.

(The picture of us in 1967)

Dawn was the first to see the Lee Generals banner waving in the air at the top of the stadium behind the Bellaire fans. "Oh, wow! How cool," she yelled, pointing toward the banner.

In a matter of seconds, dozens had seen the event taking place.

Lance, Brent and Walter yelled with excitement. By now hundreds of Lee fans were on their feet. The boys never dreamed the audience response would be so monstrous and were amazed when the Lee side of the stadium roared with excitement while pointing to the banner. The response was deafening and sent a chill up their spines. The boys had succeeded in their adventure beyond their wildest dreams.

Now a stadium of Lee fans were hysterical and continued to roar their approval. The students, players and cheerleaders continued their screaming frenzy, while it seemed not a sound came from the Bellaire side.

Coach Turner stared at the Lee banner and managed one of his infrequent smiles. "Renfro," he muttered.

Joyce Ann and Dawn continued to point at the banner waving from the top of the Bellaire bleachers.

"Awesome!" said Joyce Ann.

Dawn said, "Oh my goodness, so that's what Lance and Brent wanted with the banner!"

Joyce Ann turned to Dawn, "Brent?"

"Yes, and Lance."

Joyce Ann turned around to see if she could see Brent and immediately spotted him. "How cool!"

Everyone on the Lee side continued to cheer. Things on the Bellaire side, however, changed rapidly.

Slowly Bellaire students turned their heads and spotted the banner. At first they were confused and stunned. To them, the prank was not funny and they became angry. Many jumped to their feet and charged the three intruders.

Lance, Brent and Walter were not prepared for what they saw below them. Their smiles disappeared in an instant.

Walter's terrified eyes said it all, but his words described it best. "Oh no!"

Brent confirmed what Walter thought. "They're going to kill us!"

Lance glanced all around for an escape. He found it behind him—about ten feet below was the roof of the restrooms. He pointed and yelled, "Jump! Jump!"

Lance jumped from the stadium to the roof of the restrooms below. Walter and Brent hesitated, threw the banner over and glimpsed once more at the unhappy Bellaire fans charging toward them. They were not far behind Lance.

All three scrambled from the roof only to run into three security guards who had been alerted and saw the trio jump from the stadium. The guards rounded them up as the boys lowered themselves from the roof. They were escorted away, much to the disappointment of the angry Bellaire Cardinal fans.

Inside the security office Lance, Walter and Brent huddled together. To them it seemed as though the wait was forever. They could hear the football game continue and cheers from the fans on both sides, but had no idea what was happening. Eventually the game ended. Soon the fans began to exit the stadium and cars drove away. Finally no more sounds came from the empty stadium.

A few minutes later the lead officer for Delmar Stadium Security walked into the office and confronted the three boys.

He glared at the youthful offenders. "What you did was stupid. We called the police and you're lucky they're not coming out. We're gonna call your parents and have them come over here and get you."

Lance snickered, but Walter and Brent were terrified.

"No, not our parents. Anything but our parents," Walter pleaded.

"Believe me, it's the best thing," said the officer.

"Yeah, but not our parents," said Brent. "Give us to the Bellaire students but not to my parents!"

Only one thing worried Lance. "Who won?"

The guard stared at Lance and shook his head. "How can you even think about… " The phone rang and the officer snatched it from the cradle. "Yes, sir…okay…sure." He hung up and turned to the boys. "That was your principal. He wants you to come to his office Monday morning."

The boys nodded.

The officer said, "Okay, get out of here." All three charged the door, but before they could exit the officer yelled, "Hey!"

They halted and turned to face the stern guard whose frown slowly turned into a smile. "Lee won."

All three let out a whoop! Instantly they calmed down and walked sedately from the office. Once in the parking lot it was easy to find Brent's Volkswagen Van because it was the only car in sight. All three were still excited.

Brent laughed. "Man, that was a blast. I was never so scared or had so much fun in my life!"

Usually restrained, even Walter was animated. "Just awesome!"

Brent shook his head. "Now to see what plans old Chrome Dome has for us Monday morning."

***

Inside Brent's garage Lance worked diligently on a new surfboard. It was one of the orders Brent had gotten at Surfside. While Lance tackled his project he noticed Cotton, Marilyn and Dawn enter the driveway. When the group approached the garage they were surprised to see Lance. Cotton released Marilyn's hand and moved away as though he had been caught doing something wrong.

With a flashing smile aimed at Lance, Dawn asked, "Where's Brent?"

Lance jerked a thumb toward the house. "Inside."

Dawn nodded to Cotton and Marilyn. "Go ahead, I'll be there in a minute."

The two went in the house, leaving Lance and Dawn alone.

They just stood there and looked at each other. Finally she asked again, "Lance, last night at the game, how did you know where the plays were going?"

Lance tried to shrug it off. He was sincere when he said, "It's really hard to explain. I can feel it."

Dawn chuckled. "The banner. Lance, that was so outrageous."

He smiled. "Seemed like the thing to do."

"Did you get in trouble?"

"Gotta report to Principal Davis' office Monday morning."

"Everyone is saying you fired the team up and made them win."

Lance nodded. "That was the whole point of doing it."

"Oh, I also wanted to say you played a nice game the other day."

Lance felt uncomfortable and fidgeted a little.

"First time I've ever seen Jim intercepted," she added.

Making sure Cotton and Marilyn were inside, Lance turned to address Dawn. "Does Jimbo know about them?"

"No. Please keep it a secret."

"Marilyn the reason?" he asked.

Dawn nodded her head as Lance continued, "Marilyn is nice. Cotton should be happy to tell everyone he likes her."

Dawn grimaced. "Cotton will do anything Jim says."

"Now that's the problem—not Marilyn. If Jimbo doesn't like Marilyn, why do you still see her?"

Dawn appeared a little irritated. "Marilyn is my best friend."

"Good. Somebody who doesn't do what Jimbo wants."

"You shouldn't call him Jimbo. Jim is my boyfriend and he really is a nice guy."

Lance picked up the sandpaper and returned to his work on the surfboard. "Yeah, I've seen him at work. Nice guy."

She blurted, "Well at least he has a future. All you want to do is live for today!" Instantly, she regretted her words, but it was too late. The words stung Lance.

"Lance, I'm… "

Cotton, Marilyn and Brent interrupted the conversation as they entered the garage.

Brent nodded to Dawn. "Hi Dawn." He handed Lance a bottled coke.

Dawn turned to Brent. "Brent, I need to talk to you about something."

Brent shrugged, "Sure."

Marilyn, Dawn, and Brent walked out in the driveway.

Cotton hung back. "Lance, I loved the banner. Awesome. Bellaire went ape."

Lance managed a grin. "Thanks, Cotton."

"You should join the team."

The smile was replaced instantly with a touch of anger. "I don't do team sports."

Naturally curious, Cotton asked, "Why? You're one of the best defensive backs I've ever seen."

Again Lance smiled. "Better than Curtis?"

"Yep. Better than Curtis."

"You did a great job coming back and winning the game."

Cotton smirked. "Your banner got us going and some of Coach Turner's defensive changes really helped."

Curious, Lance asked, "Defensive changes?"

"Yeah, at halftime Coach Turner said he was going to spread the linebackers and have the cornerbacks help Curtis. It worked great."

Lance smiled, knowing that although Turner had not responded, he apparently heard every word said that night and made the suggested changes. Reflecting about that and many other things, Lance continued to observe Cotton. He could no longer hold back his thoughts.

"You're lucky to have someone like Marilyn."

Cotton was nervous and begged, "Don't tell anybody. Please?"

Lance shook his head and locked eyes with Cotton. "I won't. But if Marilyn was my girlfriend I'd tell everybody."

Uncomfortable at the conversation, Cotton squirmed. He was saved when Brent, Marilyn and Dawn returned.

Dawn said, "Well, we better go." She turned toward Lance, "Bye, Lance."

Still hurt, Lance looked away and said, "Yeah, see ya."

His reaction hurt Dawn. She hoped he would look at her, but Lance focused on the board. He didn't glance up. She turned and walked away with Cotton and Marilyn.

Lance stopped working and watched her leave. He regretted his words and was about to holler after her when Brent, all excited at the information he had received from Dawn, started rambling the story to Lance.

"Man, you won't believe it."

Lance turned to Brent. "What?"

Just as he turned, Dawn glanced back at Lance hoping he would look at her so she could at least apologize. But he appeared to be talking about something of importance with Brent. Even so, she waited a few more moments.

"Joyce Ann wants to go out with me. She thought the banner was the bravest, coolest thing ever."

Down the driveway Dawn sighed and gave up.

"Hey, that's great," said Lance. With a slight sense of urgency he turned, hoping he might catch Dawn before she was gone. When he turned his head, she was still walking away and disappeared around the corner of the house. She never looked back.

Still excited about his date with Joyce Ann, the girl he believed to be the prettiest in school, Brent said, "We're gonna go to the Catacombs next weekend. Wanna go?"

Bummed out, Lance turned back to Brent and said, "Sure."

***

Monday morning the three boys had to face Principal Davis. Not even Lance looked forward to the meeting. On the way to the office, the students congratulated the trio for the banner. Most said it turned the game around and, amazingly, Curtis was not burned during the entire second half.

This was hard for Walter and Brent to believe, but they bumped into Cotton just before they reached the office. Although Lance had heard the story he enjoyed listening to it in more detail. Cotton explained how Turner kept the formation and when the ball was snapped the linebackers spread out dropping one back. This freed up the cornerbacks to help Curtis. On the first play the Bellaire quarterback was intercepted. After a few series the other team started using running plays and short passes, but there were no more quick scores. Coach Turner had used Lance's idea.

They entered the office and waited for the Principal. A few minutes later the secretary led them into the his office.

All three stood before Principal Davis. What did he have in store? The waiting was killing them. Davis continued to roll a pencil in his hand and just stared at them without uttering a word. Lance, Brent and Walter fidgeted.

Principal Davis laid the pencil down and folded his arms on his desk then proceeded to peer at each boy. "You could have caused a riot!"

Worried, Brent said, "Sir, we were just having fun trying to get the team spirit up."

The principal didn't appreciate the response. "There are other ways to have fun. I'm seriously considering talking to your parents."

"Don't talk to my Dad," said Brent.

Confident, Davis continued his threats. "I should talk to each of your fathers."

Irritated, Lance said, "Then call my father and tell him."

Brent and Walter were horrified. They feared their fathers and knew what would happen if Principal Davis contacted them.

"Mr. Renfro, I'll get your father in here if that's what it takes."

Lance smirked, "Yeah, sure. Tell me when you talk to him."

Again Brent and Walter were astonished at what Lance said.

Principal Davis was concerned at the direction of the discussion and wondered about the punishment that should be meted out. He really hated to contact the parents, but he had to do something to get the boys' attention. He needed a reaction of fear, something he could hold over the boys to control them and make them behave. "I should suspend you."

Brent and Walter were sick with dread.

Walter almost begged, "Please sir, a suspension would ruin my scholarship."

Now Principal Davis felt he had the boys where he wanted them. "I'm going to seriously consider a suspension." He wanted them to beg.

Not Lance. No begging for him. He was still defiant. "Then quit talking and suspend us."

Horrified, Brent and Walter turned to Lance. They were at a complete loss for words and felt doomed. Even Davis was taken back at Lance's surprising response. He forced his dominating figure toward Lance. "Do you know what a three day suspension would mean?"

Lance snickered, "Yeah, a nice vacation away from here."

Brent tried to hide a smirk, but Walter was completely horrified and blurted, "Mr. Davis, I don't need a vacation. I have a test."

Angry, Davis stared at Renfro. Inside he was frustrated. He wanted to control Lance, but it wasn't working. He did not really want to suspend them, but his choices were limited. "Mr. Renfro, you don't know how tempted I am." He hesitated. "All three of you get back to class before I change my mind. I want you to know I'll be watching the three of you for the rest of the year."

Once outside the Principal's office, they ran a safe distance down the hall where they started laughing. Walter and Brent were unable to comprehend how they had gone unpunished. This was another small victory, and the victories were becoming shockingly more frequent. Things had really changed with Lance's arrival. When they reached their lockers, they took out books for the next class. Lance gave the impression he could have cared less, but Brent was ecstatic while Walter was relieved and excited.

Brent mumbled, "Rad."

Walter was calm but confronted Lance, "You were crazy to tell old Chrome Dome to contact your father."

Lance chuckled, but Brent said, "I don't know what's so funny, but I'd hate to have my father punish me. Doesn't it scare you to think about what your father would do to you?"

With a snicker Lance responded, "Not really. My father is dead."

Both boys were stunned at first, but slowly their faces filled with wide smiles as they shook their heads.

"Lance, you really push the limit," said Walter.

A grin lit up Brent's face. "I have a feeling this is going to be an awesome senior year with you here."

***

Lance arrived late to class. He gave the teacher his excuse pass and made a point to grin at Jim as he took a seat next to Dawn. Jim glared at Lance.

The teacher approached. "Mr. Renfro, you need to turn in your homework."

Somewhat irritated at the events over the last few days he said, "I don't have it."

The teacher was upset. "You have to do your homework and turn it in."

He turned his head to face the teacher and said, "You don't

understand. I don't do homework."

The teacher was aghast. "What? Everybody does their homework."

Lance shrugged his shoulders and was firm when he said, "Not me."

There was a chuckle from some of the students. Even Jim chuckled and shook his head, but Dawn was disappointed.

"That's not acceptable," said the teacher.

"Look, when my parents get home from work at night they don't have to do homework. I don't do it either," said Lance.

Even Jim couldn't hold back. All but one snickered—Dawn was sad and concerned for Lance.

Angry at his attitude, the teacher scribbled on a pad, tore the paper off and handed it to Lance, "Take this to Principal Davis. Let's see what he wants to do with you."

Chapter 12

COACH'S CHALLENGE WORKS

After the game and throughout the weekend, Coach Turner's thoughts returned to Renfro. Lance was different from all the other students and so far Turner had not come up with a way to get the boy to face the challenge. The banner at the game had been interesting, and word had already reached him that Renfro and his two friends, Hester and Baughman, had been in on the prank to drum up team spirit. Turner had to admit that what they had done worked. Of course, the changes Lance yelled out had made a difference. Even Curtis played a more inspired form of ball.

For a moment he considered Renfro's new friends and was not really surprised at Baughman. But Hester was a real shock, for straight "A" student was not one to gamble and get in trouble. He could only remember one time Hester had ever gotten pops, in which case Turner felt bad because the boy cried before even receiving the first pop.

Hester! So simple—and it had always been there. Hester would get what Coach Turner wanted from Lance. Now if Renfro did as expected it would become apparent just how fast this newcomer could run.

***

Coach Turner gathered the class together. They were all prepared for the run, but most of the students turned to watch Lance and no longer wondered if he could beat Marvin again. They wanted to see him run against Ron and Will. Even Brent and Walter wanted to see him beat Ron and Will. However Coach Turner had another plan altogether and was about to find out if it would work.

Barking instructions, Turner said, "We're going to do the same thing again today."

The students groaned while Lance frowned and blurted, "I won't run."

Coach Turner turned to face Lance. He smiled at Renfro and the smile boded ill for all. "Mr. Renfro, did I speak to you?"

Defiant, Lance snickered, "No sir."

"Mr. Renfro, this will not involve you."

Now Coach Turner had Lance's attention. He said to the others, "Today we have a race and all the losers will get ten pops. There is only one winner. Graham, Coleman, Odoms, Baughman... and Hester."

When his name was called Walter was alarmed and began to whine, "Coach, I can't beat them!"

"Mr. Hester, I suggest you reach down and find that extra bit of desire to win. You can do it if you want."

Coach Turner walked over to the line with the five runners. Walter was almost in tears and Lance hastily saw what was happening to his friend.

Across the field the cheerleaders and the jocks stopped to observe the daily ritual. Jim and the others laughed when they saw who Coach Turner had picked for the challenge.

Cotton was curious. "What is Coach Turner trying to do?"

Others had the same thought, as they too could not guess at what the Coach intended. But Lance knew the answer, even as he stepped in front of the coach with his own challenge. He couldn't let this happen to Walter.

Lance said, "Coach, let me run for Walter."

Turner turned slowly until he faced Lance. Slowly and intentionally, he looked him over as though he could care less. "I didn't invite you to this party, Mr. Renfro."

Lance almost begged, which was something he never did. "It's what you really want. Let me run for Walter."

The coach continued to glare at Lance as though it was too late and he had already decided. Then he hesitated and rubbed his chin in false consideration. His plan and had been well thought out. "I tell you what, Mr. Renfro. To let you run for Hester will cost you ten pops even if you win."

The students grumbled. This wasn't fair. Coach Turner observed Lance and waited to see if he would get the reaction he wanted. He didn't have long to wait.

Something really bothered Lance as he cast concerned eyes upon Walter. It was more than just the pops Walter would get. It was something deep and something bad that tore at Lance's soul. Subdued, he turned to Coach Turner. "Okay."

There was more Coach Turner wanted. It was the challenge he was determined to obtain, for he was the only one there who knew what really bothered Lance. The boy didn't mind pops, so he had to make one more condition to achieve the mission. "But if you lose," he pointed at Walter, "He will still get ten pops."

This struck a chord in Brent. He didn't know what was happening or why Coach Turner was doing it, but he didn't like it at all. For the first time, Brent spoke up and was defiant. "That's not fair, Coach." He turned to Lance, "Don't do it, Lance."

A metamorphosis came over Lance. He gritted his teeth. Brent and Walter saw Mr. Hyde return. "Okay, Coach Turner. You have your race."

Coach Turner saw the same change in Lance and hoped to uncover what he believed was hidden away. "Get ready."

Lance, Will, Marvin, Brent and Ron got down on the goal line ready to run the 100 yard race. The coach had Lance where he wanted, but he also had stirred something in Brent who was angrier than ever before and ready to run with all his heart.

Ron grinned at Lance. "Sorry man. Nothing personal, but I don't want any pops."

Will nodded in agreement, "Yeah, I'm sorry to both of you 'cause I don't want no boards on my ass, either."

All three managed a little chuckle.

Lance said, "And I'm sorry for what's about to happen to the two of you."

This time Ron and Will chuckled.

Ron said, "Yeah, right."

Will said, "We have the school record. No one has ever beaten us."

Lance turned to Ron and Will and chuckled. "I think those are the same words Goliath used when he saw David coming toward him."

The smiles disappeared.

Turner said, "Can the chatter." He held up his stopwatch. "It will be on ready, set, go. Okay?"

The three runners nodded. Turner walked down to the goal line at the opposite end of the field. He stopped and turned back to the runners, and yelled, "Ready, set, GO!"

All five took off like rockets. They continued stride-for-stride for 50 yards. The jocks cheered, which rapidly changed into a roar. Ron and Lance got a step on Will. Oddly, a few paces behind Will was Brent, who kept pace with Marvin. Brent was determined not to come in last anymore. At 80 yards, Ron and Lance were still even and had two steps on Will. Only a few steps behind Will were Marvin and Brent running even.

The cheerleaders were enthralled. The jock's roaring increased! Only a few yards from the finish, Lance pulled slightly ahead and held it to the finish line!

When Lance won the race the most amazing thing happened. Silent for years and subdued by the athlete's taunts and arrogance, the students let out a roar that no one had ever heard before! The jocks gasped in shock and stunned, silent disbelief. Lance defeated Ron with a margin of less than a head at the 100 yard finish. Almost as amazing, Brent and Marvin were a virtual photo finish. It was impossible to tell who really won between those two, but it appeared Brent had beaten Marvin. For the ordinary every day students, there was no doubt. Lance and Brent had brought them victory!

This was the day the students had waited for all their lives, or at least their high school careers. Their cheers and screams of excitement were so intense and powerful that students actually ran to the windows of the school to see what had happened. The jocks were nothing more than silent statues.

Jim shook his head in disbelief. "No way."

Sue King mumbled, "He beat Will and Ron!"

A little pride and excitement was reflected in Dawn's face. "Oh my goodness, Lance won!"

Even Joyce Ann was amazed. She held her hands to her chest and jumped up and down. She had seen the race she wanted to see. "Brent beat Marvin!"

All the students mobbed Lance, but Walter and Brent arrived first. They were all whooping. It was their celebration.

Turner stared at his stopwatch in disbelief and mumbled, "They beat the state record."

The five runners were still bent over catching their breath. Walter stood next to Lance, and Brent moved in to give Lance a victory slap on the back.

Lance grinned at Brent. "Way to go! You beat Marvin. I knew you could do it."

Coach Turner hurried toward them. He was almost running, but tried to hold back his own excitement. This was a day he never in his wildest dreams ever believed he would see.

"Unbelievable. Just unbelievable! You beat them!" Walter was as relieved as he was excited, "Thanks man, you saved my tail."

Lance managed a grin and a wink in response. It appeared Lance was somehow more relieved than Walter.

Now everyone was slapping Lance on the back. He managed to stand up and smile at his friends. When he turned around, Ron and Will were standing next to him. They were stunned but had a new respect for Lance Renfro.

Ron said, "Nice run, Lance."

Will agreed. "I'm glad I got a chance to run against you." He chuckled. "I just don't want to do it again."

Lance grinned back. "You two are fast. Well, I guess it's time for the pops."

Ron frowned, "Don't remind me."

Turner had arrived, "Okay boys, to my office."

After the Coach was gone the students' celebration continued. It was a celebration that would be remembered for a long, long time.

***

Coach Turner entered his office. Brent, Marvin, Ron, Will and Lance trailed behind reluctantly. The boys stopped in front of Turner's desk while the coach retrieved his paddle. With Moses in hand, Turner turned to face them. He saw a little concern in all the boys, but Lance carried his indifference like a tattoo. For Lance, the paddle was akin to seeing an old friend and Turner knew it.

Turner tapped the paddle with his hand. Something was on his mind and it wasn't the pops. It was the race he had just witnessed. "Baughman, Odom, you can go."

"No pops?" said Brent.

Coach Turner squinted his eyes. "No pops." When the two boys turned to leave, Turner said, "Baughman."

Brent stopped and turned to face the coach. Turner had a slight smile. "Nice run today."

Surprised and excited, Brent said, "Thanks Coach."

He and Marvin exited, leaving Ron, Will and Lance with Coach Turner. When they were gone Turner turned to the three boys and scrutinized them for a moment. "I've never seen a race like that in all my life. Graham, Coleman, Renfro—all of you just broke the state record."

The boys glanced at each other with huge grins and slapped each other on the shoulders in a congratulatory manner. The grins were still there when they turned back to face Coach Turner.

With a little hesitation Will asked, "The pops?"

Turner touched the paddle with fondness and proceeded to lay it gently on his desk. He looked at the boys for a moment, but mostly he tried to figure out Lance. "I've changed my mind. Get out before I change it back."

They rushed quickly from the office and away from the paddle.

Turner shook his head and mumbled, "What on earth am I going to do with you Mr. Renfro? You don't mind the pops, and you'll take them for your friends. Whether you know it or not, you may not like team sports, but you are a team player. What on earth will it take to change you?"

***

They were still running and laughing when they reached the gym and finally stopped.

Will shook his head and grinned at the other two. "Broke the state record. How do you like that!"

Again they laughed.

Ron extended his hand. "Lance, you're an okay guy."

Lance was stunned. He took Ron's hand in an extension of serious friendship.

Even Will extended his hand. "Goes double with me."

Lance appeared a little embarrassed. "Thanks. I don't know what to say."

Ron said, "I'd be on your team any day."

Lance was at a loss for words. People had asked for him to play on their team, even demanded he play on their team, but Ron and Will, in a way, were swearing an allegiance to Lance. It was one of those rare times when a guy makes friends and shares a bond due to an unusual joint venture. Ron and Will recognized that Lance inspired anyone who came within a near proximity. Both boys now acknowledged it with a sincerity Lance had seldom seen, except with his fellow surfers.

True friendships were sworn that day.

Chapter 13

A QUARTERBACK THREAT

Lance opened the door to his locker and took out a few books for the next class. He was about to close the locker when Dawn walked up.

"Hi."

Lance peered over his shoulder and smiled. "Hi."

She was excited. "I saw you run yesterday. You should go out for track!"

Down the hall, Jim spotted Dawn and saw she was with Lance. He shoved people aside so he could get to them.

Lance became a little agitated. "I don't do sports. Besides, Ron will win for the track team. They don't need me. I've got to go."

Lance walked away leaving Dawn confused and hurt. She mumbled, "What did I do?" The words barely became a thought before someone grabbed her from behind and spun her around. She was face-to-face with another angry person. Jim glared at her.

"What are you doing with that dweeb?"

Dawn was stunned and shocked at Jim's demeanor. "I was just saying I saw him run against Ron and Will."

"Stay away from him. You're my girl. Understand?"

"I know I'm your girl." She tried to calm his anger. "Hey Jim, you wanna go to the Catacombs tonight?"

This time it was Jim who was caught off guard. He actually appeared unusually nervous. "No. I have things to do." Without another word, he spun around and walked away.

Chapter 14

THE CATACOMBS

Students from the local high schools filled the club. Most were from Lee or Lamar and mingled throughout the smoke-filled atmosphere. Waitresses rushed about in an effort to fill all the orders and collect their tips. Billy Gibbons who had played sandlot football with Brent and Lance sang *99th Floor* with his band The Moving Sidewalks.

At one table Dawn, Marilyn, Joyce Ann and Denise talked about the upcoming game. Somehow the conversation returned to the race between Lance, Ron and Will. As for Joyce Ann, she always managed to get a word in about how Brent had beaten Marvin. The girls were still buzzing over other new victories. Ron and Will had been beaten. Jim Brown had been intercepted. Lance had done both.

Joyce Ann looked around and hoped to spot Brent. Almost as an afterthought, she asked, "Where's Sue?"

Denise said, "Sue said she had some other things to do."

At the entrance to the Catacombs Brent, Walter and Lance strolled in. They searched around to see if they knew anyone. Brent peered about hopefully while Lance was more casual with his eyes. Deep down, both boys were out to find a certain girl. They spied Billy and waved while he nodded back to them. Walter nodded toward some girls and walked away.

As the two remaining boys stood near the entry, Cotton walked up behind and tapped Lance. "Hey man."

Brent and Lance turned to Cotton, who said to Lance, "I thought you were fast, but I never dreamed you could out run Ron."

Lance was uncomfortable talking about sports and didn't want to discuss it anymore, but that was all Cotton could think about. "I still can't believe it. It would be fun to see you on the team."

Again Lance's anger took control. He yelled, "Why does everybody want me on the team?"

Cotton stepped back and held up his hands. "Hey man, sorry I said anything." He spotted Marilyn and waved to her and walked away from the guys.

For the first time Brent appeared a little miffed at Lance. Actually, Brent was angry and waved his arms in the air to make his point as he spoke. "Lance, why are you so hacked off at Cotton? He was just complementing you. Look, I don't care if you ever join anything. I don't know what your problem is with sports, but when people are nice to you—be nice back!"

Lance was mortified and realized he deserved the criticism. "I'm sorry, Brent, but you just don't understand."

Still angry, Brent said, "No, I don't." He waved his finger at Lance to make his point, "But do me a favor, just for tonight. Anybody who asks you to join track or football or whatever, just say thanks but you really can't right now."

Embarrassed, Lance nodded in agreement. "Okay."

A sly grin filled Brent's face when he spied Joyce Ann. He grabbed Lance's arm and said, "Come on, follow me."

They walked over to the table and Brent whisked Joyce Ann to the dance floor. She responded as though she had waited for him all night. As he pulled her away, she flashed a victorious grin toward Denise and Dawn.

Lance pulled up a chair and slid up on the seat next to Dawn, feeling bad about their last conversation. It was awkward for him, but also for her.

He tried to raise his voice above the music. "Hi, Dawn."

Dawn returned a pleasant smile. "Hi, Lance."

He nodded across the table to Denise. "Hi, Denise."

She frowned. "Whatever." Then Denise stuck her nose in the and turned back to the people on the dance floor. Her point being made, she turned back and frowned at Dawn. "He shouldn't be here."

Taken back at the rude comment, Dawn snapped, "Denise!"

Denise glared at Lance and was about to speak when a jock walked over and led her out on the floor.

Only Dawn and Lance remained at the table. The situation was a little tense.

Dawn spoke first. "Are you still mad at me?"

The words stabbed Lance. He remembered what Brent said earlier and understood his anger had controlled and ruled over him, hurting others. He couldn't continue to let that happen and needed to change it now. But no one understood what had happened to him. He couldn't let anyone in. Still, he would try to stop directing his anger toward people who had no understanding of the situation, especially the people he truly cared about. Dawn rated among the first.

"Oh no, I was never mad at you," Lance assured.

"What was wrong?"

"It's hard to explain. Maybe I can tell you one day, but not now."

She responded with a winning smile that filled her blue eyes. "I can wait." With a twinkle that most guys could only dream of ever receiving, she added, "But wouldn't that mean thinking about tomorrow?"

Lance chuckled and rolled his head. But behind the smile, he still brooded over something… and Dawn could sense it. She was just glad it was not anything she had personally done.

Lance was reluctant to speak or think about the past, but he managed, "Things have happened to me."

"Doesn't mean you can't plan a future. What do you want to do when you graduate?"

His nonchalant shrug indicated he didn't know, or he didn't care. "Nothing. Surf."

Dawn grunted and flashed her entrancing eyes upon him. "Surely you had a dream?"

For a moment Lance grasped at a long-gone memory. "Once," he mumbled. "A long time ago."

Dawn tried to hide her excitement. She felt she was finally breaking through his steel barricade. "What was it?"

His walls began to crumble. He hesitated, then shared, "Once I wanted to be a veterinarian."

Now Dawn was excited. "Oh, that would be so cool!"

The revelation of his own words shocked Lance and it was evident in his face. He even managed a feeble smile. After all these years he had finally let down a wall. It felt good. "I never told anyone before."

Dawn was excited he had confided in her and was sincere when she said, "It's a wonderful dream, Lance."

Lance glimpsed in all directions, then finally back to Dawn. "Where's Jimbo? Do I need to run and hide?"

Dawn shook her head. "He hates that name. And no, don't run and hide. You're safe. He's not coming tonight."

Lance chuckled as she playfully poked him in the ribs. Over his shoulder and not far away she noticed Cotton and Marilyn. What she saw made her sad. Afraid of what might happen, Cotton stood a distance from Marilyn, watching her but doing nothing, afraid Jim might antagonize her.

Dawn sighed. Gradually an idea formed in her mind and she turned to Lance. "Do me a favor?"

"I'll try."

"Make Cotton dance with Marilyn."

"I can't make him, but I can give him a suggestion." Lance got up and walked over to Cotton. It was his turn to apologize. "Sorry I was upset when you came in."

Cotton shook it off. "No problem."

"You know you're a good running back. You hit hard."

"Thanks, Lance."

"Can I ask you something?"

"Sure."

"You like Marilyn, don't you?" Cotton nodded, almost reluctantly, maybe even reflecting a bit of fear as though someone would catch him.

"Ask her to dance."

Worried, Cotton said, "Jim doesn't like her."

"Cotton, Jimbo is the problem, not Marilyn. I want you to think about this. Who could you live with for the rest of your life, Marilyn or Jim? I can see him wearing a dress right now. Jimbo just doesn't look like he would make you a good wife."

Cotton could barely control his laughter. "Jim in a dress. Aw man, that's a riot." Cotton took a momentary peek toward Marilyn. "Okay, but Jim's gonna be mad when he sees me with her."

"If you really care for Marilyn, does it matter what anyone thinks? Especially Jimbo?"

For a moment Cotton reflected on Lance's words. He knew Lance was right.

Lance continued before Cotton did anything. "Besides, this is your lucky night."

"What do you mean?"

A mischievous smile filled his face. "Jimbo's not coming."

Cotton turned purposefully and walked straight to Marilyn, then took her hand and led her to the dance floor. Lance walked back and sat next to Dawn. With a slight snicker he leaned back and cupped his hands behind his head.

"Okay Cupid, let's see what happens," he teased.

Content and happy, Dawn commented, "They're so cute."

Lance took Dawn's hand. "Come on, let's dance." He pulled her out on the floor. She was only slightly reluctant.

"Oh, no I can't."

Lance chuckled, "Trust me, I have it from a reliable source that Jimbo isn't coming tonight."

Dawn was unable to stop Lance and really didn't try. They danced for a few songs. Near them were Brent with Joyce Ann and Cotton with Marilyn.

A new band, Fever Tree, played a rendition of *God Only Knows*, a popular Beach Boys song. All three couples danced close. When the song ended it didn't appear any of them wanted to release their partners. The next song was wild and fast, rock and roll. The jumping dancers crowded them out and the group decided to go back to their seats. Soon another slow song came along and all six literally rushed to the dance floor.

Lance and Dawn danced close—very close. Maybe too close. Dawn's eyes revealed being with him was more than pleasant. Lance was actually happy. The song ended but they continued to hold each other, their faces almost touching, their lips so near. Dawn pushed away but she let him hold her hand back to the table where she gave him a squeeze and smiled before she released.

"I really enjoyed the dance, Lance."

He nodded and slid in next to her.

Later, all three couples were at their table deep in conversation. The band played *Cherish,* a recent Association single.

Lance said, "Yeah, the sunsets are beautiful in California."

Dawn said, "I want to see one."

"I bet Surfside Beach is just as beautiful. Have you seen a sunrise?" asked Lance.

For a moment Dawn thought about it. "No, I never have."

Brent grinned. He had a plan. "Let's go to the beach."

Dawn was hesitant. "I have to tell my parents."

"Me too," said Joyce Ann, but she wasn't hesitant. She was eager.

"So do I," said Marilyn.

"Cool," said Brent. He added, "While we're there we can catch the submarine races."

Chapter 15

RUNAROUND SUE

In the Lee gymnasium things moved very quickly. From the girls locker room came moans and groans, but not from anyone in danger. This was the sound of two people lost in the heat of passion.

A boy kissed Sue all over her neck and she clung to him as though she would never let go. He handled her passionately as her hands moved all over him and her fingers dug in his back.

"Do you think they know?" groaned Sue.

The boy pulled away to reveal… Jim Brown. He laughed. "No, they'll never figure it out."

Sue grinned, "Oh, Jim!"

They hugged again and kissed. Unknown to either Sue or Jim, another person enjoyed their every move. Only a few feet away in the shower, Janitor Morris ogled the pair in amusement.

***

The early September morning was a little cooler than usual and the strong breeze from the Gulf of Mexico only increased the chill. Brent, Joyce Ann, Cotton and Marilyn nestled around the fire. The door to Dawn's car was open and a song drifted over the beach. Dion sang, *Run Around Sue.* The fire gave off enough warmth to make the slight chill pleasant.

Lance sat next to Dawn. Both had taken metal hangers and straightened them out as skewers for fluffy white marshmallows to hang from the end over the leaping flames of the campfire. Not far away a few crabs moved sideways and scouted about, waiting for the opportunity to move in and snatch a tidbit.

On the opposite side of the fire Cotton also poked a hanger over the fire. Nestled against him, Marilyn clung to his arm and leaned against his chest. Brent bent the last hanger into shape so it too could be used over the flames. When he finished, Brent shoved a couple marshmallows on the end and sat down next to Joyce Ann.

Diminutive flames erupted from both marshmallows at the end of Lance's hanger. He pulled it near, blowing and turning slowly so the flames made a complete charcoal covering. When both morsels were completely black, he blew out the flames and pointed it toward Dawn. She took one off the end and stuffed it in her mouth. Lance ate the remaining marshmallow and casually stuck two more on the end.

Cotton blew on his and one fell into the sand, but before he could reach down a crab moved across rapidly and escaped with the treat. Everyone laughed at the thief. The group continued to enjoy the beachside snack until the plastic bag of marshmallows was completely empty.

"When is the sun coming up?" asked Joyce Ann.

Brent checked his watch. "It won't be long now."

With the chill in the air from the Gulf breeze, Marilyn started to shake. Cotton pulled her near and rubbed her arms.

Lance whispered to Dawn, "Let's go down the beach."

She smiled at Lance. "Okay."

"We're taking a walk," he announced to their friends.

Brent and Cotton nodded to Lance. The girls said nothing.

Lance and Dawn got up and walked toward the edge of the surf.

"You cold?" Brent asked Joyce Ann.

"Yes."

Brent stood up and extended his hand to Joyce Ann. "Come with me and let's warm up."

She took his hand and walked with him to the van, where they both climbed into the back.

Alone, Cotton reached for Marilyn and kissed her. She responded.

In the van Joyce Ann stumbled into the back, knocking papers off the sink. "I'm sorry," she said and started picking them up.

Brent waved his hand, "Don't worry about those."

Joyce Ann noticed someone had painstakingly hand-lettered words. Closer scrutiny revealed poetry and at the bottom of each Brent had signed his name. She asked, "You wrote these?"

Embarrassed, Brent tried to take them away from her. "They're nothing, give them back."

She pulled them away and held them where he couldn't reach, then proceeded to flip through the poems. They were good and Joyce Ann knew it. Brent kept trying to reclaim them, but Joyce Ann exclaimed, "Just let me read one."

Finally Brent relented. "Oh, okay."

Joyce Ann browsed through the dozens of poems and finally stopped at one with the title of "Live For Today, 1967." She read it aloud:

Come with me back in time,
When things were so fine.

It was a different scene,
As we listened to Jan and Dean,

With their music we hung ten in the surf.

We still played football on real turf.

It was a time to smile.
Remember the quarter mile?

That Chevy SS 396,
Really gave us some kicks.

Oh, what a time,
When we cranked up the 409

But the car that was mine,
Was the Mustang 289.

It was nasty, not really very nice,
When the game was played in snow and ice.

Neither team had any slackers,
As the Cowboys were beaten by the Packers.

The Cowboy fans shed many a tear,
But it was the same thing the following year.

Then came the military draft,
But none of us laughed.

The Beatles said, "I Feel Fine."
Somehow we always found time.

With Friday night lights,
We were up for the fight.

In California the Beach Boys were king,
And surfing was the thing.

There was nothing so cool,
As "Be True to Your School."

In Texas it was football,
We all stood tall.

Your father said, "You were born,
to be a Texas Longhorn."

We were rough and ready,
Tuff and steady.

But we listened to Rock and Roll, even Fever Tree,
It was best of times, can't you see?

The Byrds, Turtles, and Doors,
We played their music and still wanted more.

They called it the amazing race,
U.S. versus Russia; who'd be first in space?

Then there was talk that soon,
A man would walk on the moon.

The Grassroots sang "Live For Today."
That was it, there's nothing more to say.

It was like a little bit of heaven,
Back in the year 1967.

Stunned, Joyce Ann mumbled, "It's beautiful, Brent."

"Aw, it's nothing."

She shook the papers at him. "It is something, Brent. These are good."

Brent shrugged as Joyce Ann put the poems down gently on the sink. She turned around. "What did you mean in the poem when you said *real turf*?"

"The Astrodome."

"The Astrodome?"

"Yeah, it's not real grass."

Fascinated at the story, Joyce Ann admitted, "I didn't know that."

Brent shrugged, "Real grass won't grow in the Astrodome, so Judge Roy Hofheinz had a company called Chemstrand make a synthetic turf to play the games on."

Flashing a hypnotic smile she put her arms around his neck, "You're so smart." She kissed him and he happily kissed her back. After a moment, the two pulled apart.

"What are submarine races?" she asked.

Brent started laughing.

***

Down the beach, Dawn and Lance walked along the ocean edge. He took her hand in his. She didn't resist and took his arm and squeezed closer.

"Lance, what are submarine races?"

He chuckled, "There aren't any. A guy uses it as an excuse to make-out with a chick."

Dawn grinned and gazed back at the fire. She saw no one. "I'll bet if we went back we'd find out it worked."

Lance nodded in agreement and laughed.

"Next weekend a bunch of us are going to Garner State Park. You should come with us. Do you know where it is?" asked Dawn.

Lance shrugged, "Yeah, near Concan." For a moment he reflected on the past. "I used to go there with my parents."

"Everyone from Lee goes there," said Dawn.

"Yeah, it's a place I'd enjoy seeing again."

"Cool. I think it will be a lot of fun."

Dawn peered out to the horizon. The colors changed to brilliant shades of blues, reds, and slight orange. "It's beautiful."

"I know. I love the ocean."

The sun peeked over the horizon shooting shards of red and orange across the sky.

She said, "I understand why."

The breeze was cool and Dawn shivered. Lance took off his windbreaker, put it over her shoulders and wrapped his arms around her. She laid her head on his shoulder and together they gazed at the sun as it came out of hiding and slowly crept above the horizon.

* * *

The sun had not been above the horizon long when Lance and Dawn returned to their little camp. Cotton and Marilyn were asleep on a blanket with a cover pulled over them. Inside the camper Joyce Ann had managed to make coffee on an old Coleman gas stove while Brent slapped together a half dozen peanut butter and grape jelly sandwiches. He passed them out as fast as he finished them.

Dawn took three and went to wake Cotton and Marilyn. She gave each of them a sandwich and the group sat upon the blanket to eat their impromptu breakfast. Above them seagulls gathered quickly hoping to grab a crumb or two.

Inside the van Joyce Ann poured the coffee. Brent had finished off the glass jar of grape jelly and gave the last sandwich to Lance.

"You take the last one," said Lance, offering Brent his sandwich.

Brent just smiled. "You keep it. I'm gonna make a special one." He rummaged around in the drawer below the little sink and snatched a couple of candy bars. He put all but the Hershey bar back in the drawer, then laid the candy on his sandwich and munched into it.

"Eeewww," said Joyce Ann.

Brent smirked, "Try it first." He held the sandwich toward her.

She hesitated, but finally took a bite. Her eyes brightened. "This is good!"

They exited the van and a few pieces of bread fell in the sand. Lance picked them up. "I'll toss these to the seagulls." He walked over to the three sitting on the blanket. They were just finishing up their sandwiches when he arrived. He tore up the bread and started tossing pieces in the air. With their coffee in hand, Brent and Joyce Ann came over to watch the seagulls snatch the pieces in mid-flight. A few landed in the sand and the birds dared to venture near Lance.

Dawn was the first to notice. She pointed to one seagull that kept picking up bread but couldn't swallow. "Something is wrong with that one."

Cotton looked closely at the bird and saw the problem, "Bummer, it's got a fish hook in its mouth. That thing is a goner."

Lance wouldn't accept that outcome. "No. We've got to help."

Dawn agreed, "Yes, but what can we do?"

Lance looked around before figuring out how to save the seagull. He dropped to his knees, turned his head toward Dawn and said, "Throw out a few pieces until it comes closer."

She did as he said and slowly the bird inched closer.

"Throw them closer to me," said Lance.

The other three watched as Dawn coaxed the seagull closer and closer to Lance. The bird was starving. It was almost close enough when fear of its proximity to humans made it dance away and lift into the air. Yet the need to eat overwhelmed its fear. The beautiful seagull returned for the easy meal it was unable to eat.

Finally it was close enough and Lance moved swiftly yet gently, grabbing the injured seagull. When he had the bird firmly in his grasp, he noticed another problem. Not only was the hook embedded in its mouth, but the fishing line was wrapped around the bird's legs and wings.

The others moved in for a closer view.

Lance said, "Dawn, I have a knife in my pocket. Get it."

She reached in his pocket until she found the knife. She pulled it out and opened the blade.

Lance turned to Dawn. "First, I need you to pull the hook out of its mouth."

Dawn hesitated, then nodded. She tried to wriggle the hook but the bird squawked loudly. She pulled away. "I'm going to hurt it."

Lance gave her a reassuring smile and in a soothing voice said, "Sure it will hurt a little and might even bleed, but if you don't remove the hook the bird will die."

With a sigh Dawn returned to the hook, working it gently as she tried not to hurt the seagull. Her efforts were rewarded when the hook popped out. The bird squawked in relief.

Still holding the bird Lance said, "Dawn, give the knife to Brent."

When Brent had the knife, Lance instructed, "Brent, cut the line in its mouth and down near the claws."

Brent did as he was told and Lance pulled the lines away from the wing and away and out of the mouth of the seagull. Then Lance pulled up a feathered flap. "Cut the line under the wing."

Brent cut the final lines and a moment later the bird was free.

Everyone sighed. Lance grinned and put the seagull on the sand to release it. The bird hesitated and looked at Lance as though to say thanks. She spread her wings, ran a few steps and soared into the air on free wings.

"Aww, how sweet," whispered Joyce Ann.

"You saved it," said Marilyn.

Brent shook his head. "Man, you should be a veterinarian."

Lance and Dawn turned to each other and both began to laugh.

Chapter 16
MOM

Lance parked his motorcycle and walked in the front door of his duplex. He was happy for the first time in an incredibly long time. Off came his windbreaker, which he tossed on the couch.

Bob came in from the back, his face revealing tribulation. "Lance, your... "

It was evident he was lost for words.

"What?" Lance asked.

Bob shook his head. "Your mother isn't going to make it."

In shock and denial Lance backed away and shook his head, "No. That's impossible."

"I wish it was."

Lance wouldn't accept the revelation. As he raced to his mother's room, he said, "You're wrong. She'll be okay. You'll see."

Beverly rested helplessly in the bed. A needle protruded from her arm and a tube attached to the needle ran to a bottle with clear fluid hanging from a cold chrome steel stand. The nurse sat in a chair near the bed. Lance pulled up a chair, sat down and took his mother's hand. Bob stood behind him.

"How ya feeling, Mom?"

Beverly managed a feeble smile, "Pretty good, Lance."

He tried to smile brightly. "Just wait, you'll be up in no time."

A little groggy, she replied, "Uh, huh." She glimpsed into Lance's eyes and her eyes became a little brighter. "I love you, Lance."

His voice cracked, "I love you too, Mom."

***

Inside Brent's garage, everything was quiet. In the corner, Lance bent over the surfboard. Even a statue had more movement than he did. He held a piece of sandpaper on the surfboard but his eyes were transfixed in another world. He stared straight ahead.

Brent walked in, turned on the transistor radio, picked up a few thing, and almost bumped into Lance, who remained in a self-induced trance. Brent let out a yelp and jumped back. He tried to catch his breath and held his hand over his chest.

"Lance! Man, you scared the heck out of me."

Lance didn't move.

"Lance?"

He remained motionless and oblivious to Brent.

Worried, Brent walked over to him. "Lance?"

When Brent grabbed Lance's arm he finally got a reaction. Lance blinked and turned, although his eyes were vacant.

Brent was really worried. Lance behavior was really alarming, "Man, what's wrong with you?"

Lance stared straight through Brent, as if seeing past him and into another realm. Tears rolled from his eyes. "My mom... she's dying."

Chapter 17

ULTIMATUM

Inside the Corvette Jim and Dawn argued. He berated her unmercifully. The discussion was heated and Dawn found herself almost in tears.

"So you spent the weekend with this dork?"

Dawn shook her head and waved her hands in defense. "You don't understand, Jim. All of us went to the beach to see the sunrise. It wasn't a weekend."

"We're going steady and you have another date. How can you do this to me? How can I trust you?"

Sobs rolled from her chest. "It wasn't a date. Nothing happened."

"I should break up with you." His face was red with anger. He grabbed Dawn's shoulder and shook her. "Don't you ever talk to him again!"

Jim started to get out of the car, but he turned back to Dawn and threatened, "If I ever find out you were talking to him again, I'll turn him into hamburger meat!"

The threat terrified Dawn. "Oh no, please Jim, don't hurt Lance."

Chapter 18

JIM'S WORLD CRUMBLES

Huddled together in the school hall stood Jim, Sue, Mike and Bill. All were in a heated discussion. At the other end of the hall were Dawn and Cotton. Marilyn approached, but something was incredibly different in her demeanor. Cotton held onto her hand.

When Jim saw them his jaw almost hit the floor. "What's going on around here?"

Mike McClain grinned. "Looks like Cotton has a girlfriend."

Dawn smiled and said, "Hi, Jim."

Jim grunted and pushed her aside without even a word. He took a few steps to confront Cotton. Dawn was hurt and embarrassed.

Jim pulled Cotton aside where no one could hear. "What have I told you about her? Ditch the skuzz and don't bring her around us anymore."

Cotton hesitated, but only for an instant. Something surged up within him, something noble. He no longer cowered back but rather stood tall and confronted Jim. He appeared to tower over the jock, no longer submissive. The transition was swift and complete. Cotton had already made his decision and his eyes finally reflected the defiance he felt. "Marilyn is my girlfriend. I gave her my senior ring."

Brown shook his head, then lifted both hands in the air and grunted in disbelief. "Do you understand anything I've told you?"

Cotton actually smiled. He was in control and it felt good. "Yeah, Jim. I guess it means I won't be hanging around you anymore."

Abruptly Cotton walked over to Marilyn and took her hand gently in his. "C'mon, Marilyn. It's time for us to beat it."

The others were aghast and turned to see what Jim would do, but he remained a statue. His world was crumbling.

***

The halls filled with students as they raced to class to beat the tardy bell. Dawn opened her locker, put two books in, and proceeded to take a few out when Lance walked up behind her. He touched her on the back. When she turned around, he smiled.

"Hi."

Dawn was horrified as she checked in all directions to see if Jim was near. She was desperate and concerned for Lance. "Go away. Leave me alone."

Confused, Lance said, "What?"

She tried to push him away for his own safety, but he had no way of knowing.

"Leave. Don't talk to me anymore."

Lance backed away, the hurt reflected in his movement and eyes. "Sure." He turned his back on Dawn and disappeared into the throng of students.

She watched him leave. She was hurt, sad, scared and afraid as her emotions rocked back and forth. Tears filled her eyes as she pulled the last book from her locker.

Then she stopped. "What have I done?"

As she muttered these final words to herself, a hand roughly grabbed her shoulder and spun her around. Dawn stood face-to-face with an angry and peeved Jim Brown. "I told you what I'd do if I found you talking to him again."

"No, Jim. I told him to go away," Dawn begged.

Jim stormed away on a new mission.

***

A few hours later in the school hall, Lance and Brent leaned against the wall discussing things. Brent had learned from Lance there was never any hurry to get to class. He had plenty of time to make it at the one-minute warning. Living on the edge gave Brent a small thrill, but when the one-minute bell rang he was ready to dart. Lance, naturally, did not move.

Brent hesitated. "You coming?"

Kicking at the concrete floor with his tennis shoes, Lance turned to Brent. Angry and upset, he said, "I'm ditching school."

Brent could see something really bothered him, "What's wrong, Lance?"

"Things. Maybe I'll come back tomorrow."

"You still going to Garner with us Saturday?"

"I doubt it."

Lance turned and walked away.

Chapter 19

COACH TURNER REVEALS THE SECRET

Coach Turner was at the chalkboard diagramming a play for the next game when Brent walked in.

"Want me, Coach?"

Turner motioned to the chair. Brent sat down.

"What do you know about Renfro?"

Brent shrugged. "Not much. He's an unbelievable surfer. Even makes surfboards." Brent flashed a wide grin, "And I love the fact he intercepted Brown."

Turner managed a rare smile. "Yeah, I heard about that."

Brent grunted. "But you know what I like best about Lance? He's just a nice guy. His father died, and now his mother is dying."

"I know. I just found out." Turner hesitated for a moment and said, "Ever wonder why he doesn't play sports?"

"None of my business. I don't play either."

Turner squinted his eyes, "No, but why does he *hate* sports? I'm sure you've seen it."

Brent nodded. He was curious and anxious for the answer.

Coach Turner continued, "Are you his friend?"

"Yes."

"Lance won't let me in. Maybe you can get through to him."

More than curiosity made Brent ask, "What's going on Coach?"

"Does he carry a knife?"

Brent nodded and shrugged, "Yeah. I do too. So what?"

Turner continued, "The knife is a reminder of what's eating at him." Turner studied Brent, sighed, and locked eyes with his student. He was sincere when he said, "First you must know what happened to Lance. A few years ago..."

***

The halls were filled with students and a few teachers. Most of the students rushed to their next class. Near Dawn's locker she and Brent chatted.

"Lance ditched school. I saw him and he was bummed out."

Guilty and upset, Dawn said, "It's all my fault. Jim threatened to beat him up if I talked to him."

Brent looked around, hoping he might find Jim. "That jerk." He turned back to Dawn, "Did you know his mother is dying?"

Her expression said everything. "No!" Her concern was evident. "Poor Lance!"

Brent said, "There's more you should know about Lance… "

Chapter 20

ANOTHER SECRET REVEALED

The cheerleaders were dressed and almost ready for practice. Sue, Joyce Ann and Denise shook out their pompoms as they walked out of the gym. Dawn shook out her own pair and noticed one was missing. She stopped.

"Go on. I left one of mine."

The other three girls continued to the field while Dawn ran back to find her lost pompom. Seconds later she was at her locker and found her missing pompom lying on the floor under the bench. She hurried from the dressing area and into the gym, then heard voices coming from the janitor's room.

Dawn heard Morris, the janitor, laugh and speak rather loudly.

"Yeah, the quarterback," he said.

His comment caught her attention. There was only one quarterback at Lee—her boyfriend. She not only stopped to listen, but crept toward the janitor's room to hear more clearly.

"He gets a heavy case of lip-lock with that blonde cheerleader almost every night," said Morris. Again he laughed.

Dawn froze. She felt numb and dazed. With her ear nearly pressed against the door, she listened in despair to the entire conversation.

The janitors took their mopping materials from the closet as Morris continuing with his story.

"They sneak in, and I usually step in the shower and watch."

"No kidding? The quarterback?" said Vincent.

"Yeah, the quarterback, that Jim Brown fella. They're an item, he and that blond. He'll probably be here again tomorrow night. You can set your watch to those two."

Dawn stopped breathing for a second, stunned and heart broken. She ran from the gym as both men laughed uncontrollably. Then she broke into tears as she charged on the field, but she ran away from practice. She couldn't face the other cheerleaders now, especially Sue.

Chapter 21
THE FIGHT

The gold custom Honda 350 rolled to a stop on the side of Brent's garage. Lance cut the engine and put the kickstand in place. Sliding from the leather seat he strolled toward the garage door. He was caught completely off guard, neither alert nor prepared, when Mike and Bill stepped out to block him. From behind Jim moved swiftly and shoved Lance off the concrete and onto the grass where he rolled to a stop.

Lance turned to face the three boys. Although he knew he was in trouble, he remained defiant and grinned at Jim.

"Jimbo. What a surprise. And it's not even my birthday."

Jim was ready for the challenge. "Okay, smart ass, get up."

Again Lance gave Jim a defiant smirk. "Beats being a dumb ass like you."

"Get up! I'm going to enjoy this," screamed Jim.

Lance pulled himself up from the ground and stood erect. He glared at Mike and Bill. "Are you two just a couple of puppets? What, you just let Jimbo pull your strings? You going to do his dirty work, too?"

This wasn't going anything like Mike and Bill expected. They failed to respond.

Jim didn't care. "I'm going to kick your butt!"

Lance turned back to face Jim. "What does that prove, Jimbo? You're a tuff guy?"

"That's the last time you call me Jimbo."

Jim charged Lance, who swung in defense. But Jim parried the blow and responded with a powerful punch to Lance's stomach. Lance crumbled to his knees and gasped for breath. Jim bounced and paraded on his feet in the vein of a professional boxer ready to give Lance more. He laughed to Mike and Bill, "He can swim and run, but he can't fight." He turned back and stared fiercely at Lance. "Get up, coward."

Lance turned his face and glared at each of the boys. Angry and even more bold, he pointed to each. "Coward? Each of you are the reason I don't play sports. Your kind hurts the weak. You destroy lives. You are, and will be, bullies for the rest of your lives. Look at yourselves."

Surprised and alarmed, Bill and Mike actually looked at each other.

"What do you see? It's not good. All three of you are evil. Me? A coward?" questioned Lance. He pointed at Jim. "Jimbo, you're the coward."

There was no hesitation in Jim's fist when he snapped a wicked right to Lance's face and knocked him flat on his back.

"Don't call me Jimbo!"

All Lance could do was groan. Slowly, he rolled to his stomach and managed to pull himself to his knees. He spit blood from his mouth and staggered to his feet. Still defiant, he spread his arms wide leaving his stomach open. "C'mon football hero, give me your best."

He didn't need another invitation. Jim gave him his best shot, but this time Lance dodged the blow and managed to hit Jim in the nose. A trickle of blood escaped from Jim's nasal cavity.

Jim went berserk and responded with a fist to the stomach followed instantly with another to Lance's nose. Again he knocked Lance to the ground. Lance withered in pain but managed to get to his knees as blood oozed from his nose and lips.

"Stay away from Dawn," Jim demanded.

Lance managed a feeble smile. *So the bully's thoughts were on Dawn?* The strange anger returned. "No, Jimbo."

Enraged, Jim moved swiftly and hit Lance in the body again and again until Lance fell to the ground. Lance struggled to his knees. One eye puffed up.

Intentionally Lance said, "I love Dawn."

"Shut up!" Jim screamed, losing control. He pummeled Lance as hard as he could causing Lance to hit the ground.

Still on his knees, Lance wobbled and managed to get to his feet and face Jim. The injured eye was almost swollen shut. More insubordinate than ever, Lance grinned. "I love Dawn."

A quick fist to the body knocked Lance to the ground once more. Lance rolled over and got to his hands and knees. It was obvious Lance was intentionally antagonizing Jim. "Nothing you do to me will ever change what I feel for Dawn."

Mike was concerned. "Jim, you need to stop."

Lance wasn't finished with his verbal attack. "When you finish with me, you will have lost."

This was too much for Jim. He became a monster. He reached over and jerked Lance to his feet and started to pound him without mercy until Lance appeared to be unconscious.

Both Mike and Bill grabbed Jim.

"Stop Jim! Stop!" yelled Jim.

"Jim, cool it," advised Mike.

Jim released the feeble and weak body, which crumbled into a bloody pile on the grass. Lance groaned and moaned.

Bill and Mike tried to restrain Jim, but he still managed to hover over Lance and scream, "I won! I won!"

Lance struggled to get up but was unable. He managed to mumble, "You lost... Jimbo. You lost."

Out of control, Jim tried to beat on Lance even more. If not for Bill and Mike, Jim might have permanently injured Lance or even killed him, but somehow they managed to drag the unhinged jock away.

Unexpectedly the lights outside the garage flickered, then lit the area around the combatants. Somebody released the latch from inside the garage. Lance fell over and rolled to his back.

"Beat it!" hissed Bill to his buddies.

Mike said, "Scram!"

All three ran from the scene of their attack just as the garage door swung open.

Brent stepped out the door and peered about to find the source of the noise. He saw nothing until he heard a moan. Glancing in the direction of the helpless sounds, he saw Lance. He ran and knelt to the injured body on the ground.

"Lance! Are you okay?"

Semiconscious, Lance mumbled, "I love you, Dawn."

Brent shook his head and assisted Lance to his feet.

***

Lance sat on the kitchen countertop and grimaced as Brent cleaned his face. A steak covered Lance's eye.

"Man, you got nailed bad. You should go to the doctor."

"I'll be okay."

"No, you're not okay."

Lance tried to smile but his face hurt as he groaned. "Been hurt worse. In Malibu I went over the falls big time, ate a Neptune Cocktail and finished it off with a sand facial. Nothing's worse than that."

Brent looked intently at Lance's face from one side to the other, which resulted in a frown. "From the look of your face it couldn't have been much worse. What about Jim?"

Lance pulled the steak off his eye, "Jimbo? I'm more concerned about Dawn."

Brent shook his head in dismay. He was really worried about Lance. "Man, stay away from Jim."

With a deep sigh Lance nodded in agreement, "Yeah, but he came after me."

Brent shook his head, "The guy is a nut case."

Lance laughed and squinted, for his eye still smarted. Brent reached to reclaim the steak. "Sorry, I gotta get that back in the icebox. My Old Lady is gonna cook it tomorrow night."

"Nothing like a little seasoning," said Lance.

Both boys laughed as Lance peeled the meat off his face and returned it to Brent.

Chapter 22

DAWN LEARNS THE TRUTH

The halls of Robert E. Lee High School were filled to capacity. Brent walked alongside Dawn.

"Lance wasn't in class. Have you seen him?"

"The teacher in his homeroom made him go to the nurse's office. He got beat up pretty bad last night."

Again Dawn showed her sincere concern. "What happened?"

Brent made a face. He was angry. "Ask your boyfriend. I gotta go." He turned and went up the stairs while Dawn continued to her class.

When she arrived at her next class she peered inside, satisfied with what she saw. She waited next to the door and wasn't disappointed, because she soon saw Jim parading toward her. His entourage surrounded him and among them were Mike and Bill. When they reached the door to the class, Dawn said, "Jim."

He stopped while the others continued into the classroom.

"Did you have a fight with Lance?" Dawn asked.

Proud of what he had done, Jim responded arrogantly, "Yeah. So what? He thinks he's a hot shot. Well, he isn't so tuff. I pounded his cocky little face. He got what he deserved for messing around with you."

Dawn continued, "So if you mess around on me, can I have the team…" She took a moment to look at the team players in the classroom. Dawn sneered and made an emphasis on her next words, "... POUND you?"

If looks could have killed, Dawn seriously wounded Jim. For the first time she had the upper hand. For the first time, Jim felt minuscule and uncomfortable.

Caught completely off guard, he squirmed uneasily and didn't have an immediate comeback. Stumbling over his words he said, "You're my girl. I don't do things like that."

Dawn gave no indication she believed him, "Promise?"

He almost choked, "Uh, yeah."

They continued to stare at each other until the bell rang. Dawn turned and went into the classroom. Guilty as sin, Jim just stood there.

Chapter 23

TURNER GIVES LANCE AN OPTION

Coach Turner sat at his desk going over play diagrams for practice that afternoon. While he worked them up Lance walked into his office.

"You want me, Coach?"

The first thing Turner noticed when he looked up was the swollen eye. "I'd like to talk to you, Renfro." In addition to the black eye, Lance had a cut on his lip and cheek. Turner studied the injuries. "Been in a fight?"

Lance pointed to his face. His anger and hostility returned. "Things like this are why I will never play sports again. I won't join the team."

Turner shook his head and sighed, indicating he could care less. He waved Lance off, "Didn't ask you to."

Still suspicious, Lance calmed down. Now he was a little confused. They always wanted him to play. "You don't want me to join the team?"

"No," Turner answered firmly, then paused to stare at Lance long and hard. "Oh, it would be nice, but my players all want to play. I won't have anybody on my team who doesn't want to play. If you don't want to be on the team, I don't want you." Again Turner paused for effect and observed Lance intently. "Only a bully forces you to do what you don't want to do. Am I correct?"

This only intensified Lance's suspicions. He was about to respond, but Turner held his hand up.

"Hold it, Renfro. First I want to show you something."

Turner stood up and walked from his office with Lance close behind. They moved down the hall until they reached the football team's locker room. Turner continued inside and as though on a mission, moved straight toward the front of a locker and opened it. Turner stepped aside so Lance could see what was strategically placed.

A team jersey hung inside the locker along with a pair of pants. On the shelf was a helmet. Cleated shoes and socks were on the bottom shelf. The locker contained a complete football uniform.

Turner monitored Lance's reactions closely. "If you ever change your mind, this is for you." He put emphasis on his last words, "But, only if *you* want it."

Helpless, all Lance could do was stare into the locker. As though in a trance he pulled the jersey off the hanger and held it before him. The number "43" was emblazoned on the back and just above the number was the name "RENFRO." Tears filled his eyes. He couldn't take his eyes off the jersey. The words chocked in his throat and he was barely able to whisper, "It's his number."

Satisfied, Coach Turner folded his arms across his chest. "That's right."

Lance glared at Turner. "You know!"

"Yes, I know and I understand. But don't waste your life trying to live for today. Remember: Without faith there is no hope. Without hope there is no tomorrow."

Lance's emotions shifted back and forth from anger to sadness to rage as swiftly as thunder and lightning.

Serious and firm, Turner said, "Don't wear that jersey unless you want to play." Without waiting for a response, he spun around and walked from the dressing room, leaving Lance alone.

In the privacy of his thoughts and tragic memories, Lance collapsed to the bench and squeezed the jersey to his chest while the tears flowed. Lance cried hard, very hard.

Chapter 24
EXPOSED

Robert E. Lee High School was closed for the day. Evening had set in and only a few teachers remained in the workroom to check test papers. In the auditorium a group of students practiced for an upcoming play. In the girl's locker room two students carried out a routine ritual. The lights were out all throughout the bathrooms and students were forbidden access after-hours.

Jim Brown groped Sue King. She eagerly accepted his advances and tore at him to get his shirt off. Sue and Jim kissed passionately as they pulled at each other's garments.

Abruptly while caught in the heat of passion, the lights flashed on and the startled couple jumped. As Sue screamed and Jim spun around, it was like someone had knocked their breath away when they caught sight of Dawn nonchalantly leaning against the wall with her hand still on the switch.

Sue gasped. Jim jumped as though prodded with electricity. The convicted boyfriend began to scramble and button his shirt.

Calm like nothing had really happened, Dawn said, "Hi, Sue. Practicing for the game?"

Horrified beyond belief, Sue was unable to respond. Frantically she tried to button her blouse while hiding behind Jim.

Jim gathered his wits, then displayed his arrogant pride and swagger like a brand. He even squinted his eyes and frowned at Dawn as though she had done something wrong. "What are you doing here?"

The absurdity of his words was a slap in the face. Dawn could not believe what she heard. She managed to snicker, "I should be asking you that question. Remember your promise to me today?"

Dawn tried to look over Jim's shoulder at Sue, who was completely humiliated and wanted to crawl away and hide.

Dawn continued to stare. "My friend," she said to her traitorous fellow cheerleader.

As always, Jim tried to dominate the situation just as he had in the past. His habit was to shift blame and make others look bad. "You have no business being here!"

The threats continued as Dawn grew even more incredulous at Jim's attitude. An apology was due, yet he responded with insults. If only Jim showed a little regret... but in his mind, he still believed he was right. She could see this more clearly now, especially in this situation. Even so, she was hurt and angry.

"You're not even sorry." She gritted her teeth "You lying jerk!"

Dawn twisted Jim's senior ring off her finger and threw it at him. He ducked and the ring bounced around the locker room and rolled into the shower stalls.

Jim was haughty. "You can't do this to me. You belong to me."

Dawn managed to laugh. "You don't own me."

Jim was still angry. "That rat-fink told you just to get even."

A slight smile lit up Dawn's face. "Lance? Because you beat him up?" For a moment a comparison of Lance and Jim rolled around in her mind. It was so clear now. "No, it wasn't Lance. He has honor—something you know nothing about." Dawn flashed a wicked smile and cast knowing eyes toward the showers. "Morris, come out or I'll get the principal."

Horrified at the thought of another person observing them, Sue managed to snag her last button and turned in wide-eyed shame at the showers.

Not a sound could be heard.

Dawn repeated, "Morris!"

A slight shuffle came from the showers. Morris inched out and poked his head out of the shower stall.

Sue tried to cover up and hid her face with her hands. "Oh, my god!"

Morris stepped out completely.

Jim mumbled, "No way."

Morris pleaded, "Please don't tell the principal."

Dawn waved them off. "The three of you can discuss that." She turned and stormed from the girl's locker room as tears filled her eyes. She could hear all three jabbering frantically. As she walked across the gym she wiped away the tears.

From the girls locker room Jim hurled another insult at his former girlfriend. "It's your fault!"

For the first time since Dawn had dated Jim, there was relief in her eyes.

Jim screamed again, "You would never do it with me! It's your fault!"

Dawn sighed, happy it was over. A new skip found its way in her stride. As she reflected on the end of her relationship with the school's quarterback, gradually wonderful thoughts filled her mind.

Chapter 25

GARNER STATE PARK

Brent carried a trashcan to the front of the street and placed it near the curb. He turned and walked toward his van. A Honda rumbled around the corner and roared up. Brent waited near the door of his van for Lance, who rolled to a stop next to him.

Lance turned off his engine. "My mother is sick. I'm ditching school again today."

Brent asked, "Going to the game?"

Shaking his head vigorously Lance said, "Nope. I'm hacked at the Coach."

"Coming to Garner?"

"Nope."

A slight smile creased Brent's lips, "You should, unless you're stupid."

Lance cocked his head to the side and eyed Brent, curious. "What do you mean?"

Brent grinned, "Haven't you heard the news? Dawn broke it off with Jim. He's history."

Lance's eyes brightened. This changed everything as a slow, knowing grin filled his face. "What a dork. He had it made. He sure blew it."

"So let me ask you again. You going to Garner?"

"Yeah, I'll be there. Not even a crazy quarterback can stop me now."

They both chuckled. Lance pushed the starter button, revved the engine on his Honda, and turned his head to Brent. Instantly, his whole persona changed. "Thanks, Brent. Well, I'm gonna cut out."

The Honda roared away.

***

It was late in the afternoon at Neal's Cabin Resort. On the Frio River near the swing, Lance sat on his Honda and looked intently at the steps leading to the rope where he had met Angel. *I'll never forget you, Angel…* Content with current events, he no longer had to cling to a dream. *I've found somebody else.*

He started the Honda and smiled as he rumbled off toward Garner State Park only a few miles away.

***

Students from high schools all over the state had gathered at Garner State Park for a weekend of rock and roll, dancing, and drinking. A few bands had gathered to play their favorite music. One band set up next to the stone dance area near the river. Students continued to arrive and fill the park. Most clustered with friends from their schools. Some meandered around, meeting people from other schools. Boys prowled for that perfect dream gal and girls searched for their ideal romantic hunk.

In one nearby huddle were the students from Houston's Robert E. Lee High School: Dawn, Brent, Cotton, Walter, Joyce Ann, Denise, Marilyn, Ron, Will, Marvin, some of the jocks and other girls hoping to catch some of the available ones. They stood together talking about football and music. Mostly, the crew just engaged in a good time.

Dawn, Brent, Joyce Ann and Marilyn talked.

"Do you know if he's coming?" Dawn wondered.

"He said he would."

Dawn continued to scan the parking area for Lance.

The sun was low in the western sky when she heard the familiar rumble from the Honda 350. She turned to see Lance roll into the parking area and ran to greet him. He had just climbed off the seat when she came up from behind.

She slowed to a walk. "Hi."

Lance spun about and grinned. He still had a few cuts on his face and his eye was a little black. Dawn was surprised to see the marks from the fight.

"Hi, Dawn."

She pointed to his face. "Is that what Jim did to you?"

Lance rubbed his cheek and eye. "Yeah, that Jimbo is one heck of a fighter. He kicked my butt."

"Well," Dawn smiled and chuckled, "Jimbo is history." They both laughed some more.

Lance was sincere when he said, "I'm sorry for you, Dawn, really. But... "

"But what?"

"He was a fool and I can't say that I'm sad you're not with him."

Again, Dawn laughed. She took Lance's arm and pulled him toward the others. "I'm just a free spirit now."

"A pretty one, too."

Dawn's face turned a slighter shade of red. With Lance in tow, she clung to his arm, "How is your mother?"

With a sigh of relief he replied, "She's doing better. That's why I came up here."

"Great."

Oblivious to their surroundings, the two had already walked into the middle of their group. Cotton, Brent, Ron, Will, Marvin, Joyce Ann and Marilyn surrounded them, all happy to see Lance. The guys greeted him with a pat on the shoulders or a gentle nudge.

With an arm around Marilyn, his official girlfriend, Cotton Dickey said, "Good to see you, man."

Lance patted Cotton on the shoulder. "Same here, Cotton."

Grinning from ear to ear, Cotton said, "I told everybody about Marilyn. I have you to thank."

Lance understood. "No, Cotton, you did it. No one else." He glanced at Marilyn and grunted at Cotton, "Feels good doesn't it?" The good feeling was also reflected in Marilyn's face.

Dawn still clung to Lance's arm. It didn't appear she would ever let him go.

"It feels great, Lance," agreed Cotton.

Brent broke through with a beer and gave it to Lance "Welcome to Garner State Park."

They tapped their long neck beers together and the bottles foamed over. They were quick to chug a little so as not to lose any of the precious brew. When the flow came to a stop they broke out laughing.

The group congratulated Dawn and Lance, but most talked about the Jim Brown and Sue King situation. It appeared that neither Jim, Sue or Morris intended to do anything and just hoped it would die down. But the locker room scandal had been the talk of the school. Jim and Sue were so mortified both refused to go to Garner State Park. No "Jimbo" and no "Runaround Sue," as the students had begun to call the two. Some students had even gone as far as to hum Dion's song when they passed Sue in the hallways. A few called Jimbo the "Quarterback Sneak."

While the group talked Brent was the first to see Mike and Bill approach. The two boys walked toward Lance. Cotton, Ron, Will and Marvin, along with most of the other jocks, gathered around Lance in a protective manner.

The jocks protected him! Lance was stunned. Nothing like that had ever happened.

With their heads hung low, Mike and Bill stopped in front of Lance. Dawn continued to cling to Lance as if to show he was hers and also to form more of the protective barrier.

Lance sneered at them. "Looks like the Goon Squad has arrived."

Some of the jocks laughed. Mike and Bill were embarrassed and both turned crimson. Lance intentionally checked behind as if he expected to see someone—namely, Jim. He turned back to Mike and Bill. Their heads hung low.

Lance continued, "So where's Jimbo? Do I get another beating?"

Mike and Bill saw their fellow players lined up against them. They understood and were upset and thoroughly mortified.

Bill was sincere when he apologized. "Sorry, Lance."

Mike nodded. "We deserved that."

Dawn was angry. "How could you do that to Lance?"

They shrugged. They didn't really know how to respond, for there was no excuse.

Lance broke the ice. "Actually, you might say they saved me." Stunned at Lance's comment, Mike and Bill looked up at him. With a snicker, Lance added, "Jim would have killed me it they hadn't gotten him off me."

Mike and Bill managed feeble grins. Mike said, "Bill and I talked it over. We came to tell you we're sorry for what we did." Something else was really eating at him. "And we're not his puppets."

Bill agreed. "Yeah. That will never happen again. If there is ever trouble, we're with you."

Lance was stunned as Mike and Bill extended their hands. He shook each firmly.

Mike grinned. "You're an okay guy, Lance."

Bill said, "I'd have you on my team anytime."

"You taught us a valuable lesson," admitted Mike.

Lance smiled and nodded. "Thanks."

***

The party at Garner State Park was in full swing. The band rocked. Many danced, while most had broken down into smaller groups of really close friends. Lance and Dawn danced together as did Cotton and Marilyn and Brent with Joyce Ann.

On the cut stone dance floor Dawn clung to Lance. Both were content and happy.

"There's a place near here, Concan, where my parents used to go for the summer," said Dawn.

Lance reflected and remembered. "Neal's Cabins?"

"Yeah, how did you know?"

"Been there."

"I love it."

He loved it too. "Best memories of my life... until now."

Dawn stopped dancing and peered deeply into Lance's eyes. She was excited. "I want to go there now and show you my favorite place!"

Chapter 26
THE SWING

Somehow Dawn talked Cotton, Marilyn, Brent and Joyce Ann into joining her and Lance on their venture to Neal's Cabins.

Dawn grabbed Lance's hand and they walked ahead of the other four. Marilyn and Cotton tried to keep up, but fell back. Brent and Joyce Ann were more than content to drop way back out of sight.

Lights hung in the cypress trees lit up the river and the path. Dawn and Lance held hands as they continued toward their destination, then slowed a little. Dawn took the opportunity and moved away from the trail toward a huge, tall cypress at the edge of the river. She leaned against the trunk and again glanced back up the river. Assured none of their friends were near, she flashed an enticing smile with her hypnotic eyes. Lance moved near her.

"We have some time. I don't see them yet." She stared through him, taking him under her spell. She reached out and pulled him near. He trapped her with a hand on each side against the gnarled cypress. She put her hand on his chest. Lance bent forward until his lips touched hers. He kissed her gently. She put her arms around him and pulled him closer. They kissed again, then pulled apart just slightly. She laid her head on his chest and he wrapped one arm around her.

Dawn sighed. "Lance, I'm so happy."

He couldn't remember the last time he was this happy. "So am I, Dawn." Things seemed so different than just a few months before.

"The best memories of my life are here and you just made them better," said Dawn. She was radiant.

Down the river Marilyn and Cotton ambled toward them. Dawn pushed Lance away and took his hand. "C'mon, I want to show you something."

Onward they trekked to her surprise destination. Her arm wrapped tightly around Lance, whose arm was draped snugly over her shoulders.

"I want to show you what used to be my special place on the river," said Dawn.

"Sure," said Lance. He didn't really care where she took him just as long as he was with her. The river was so familiar, yet it seemed a lifetime ago when he had walked along the same trail.

"Did you have a favorite spot here?" Dawn asked.

"Once I did."

"I want you to show it to me after you see mine."

They were so happy. Dawn almost danced with excitement. For a moment, she was the little girl who had played on the river all over again.

"Okay, Dawn."

"Quick, let's get Marilyn. She and I always used to play there."

When Cotton and Marilyn finally caught up with them, Dawn took Marilyn's hand. They darted ahead and jumped around like two excited little girls with secrets they were about to reveal.

Lance sighed. She reminded him so much of Angel, but that was a lifetime ago. Now he had Dawn. Once again he reminded himself that he could let go of Angel.

Marilyn was excited. "Remember the swing?"

When they came upon it Lance was stunned. This was the same swing where he met Angel! Could her favorite spot also be the one he cherished so much in his own heart?

Dawn grabbed Lance and pulled him up the steps. Mechanically, he grabbed the rope.

She warned Lance, "Don't be jealous, but I want to tell you about a boy I met."

"Sure."

Marilyn and Cotton drew near. Marilyn already knew the story but it was fun to hear it again. Brent and Joyce Ann walked up to listen.

For a moment, Dawn tried to remember exactly what had happened. "He said he would come to the dance but he didn't. Still... "

With Dawn's revelation, astonishment held Lance's attention. *Could it be?*

He said, "Maybe he got hurt."

Dawn managed a laugh. "Maybe. He was so cute. Marilyn and I watched him swing."

Marilyn put her hand to her mouth and gave Lance a strange look. There was something about him. Now she could see it in his face.

Dawn continued, "He never would look at us. But when he did see me, he was standing right where you are now." She turned to Marilyn, "He was where Lance is, wasn't he Marilyn?"

Marilyn continued staring at Lance with her mouth wide open, and Dawn finally noticed. She furrowed her brows at Marilyn and wondered what bothered her, but it didn't matter. She was determined to finish her story. "Then he gave me... " She turned back to face Lance, who held the rope toward her. His eyes welled up.

"... the rope."

She took the rope, but now all she could do was stare. She saw what Marilyn saw. Lance and Dawn gazed at each other in disbelief. Dawn reached up and touched her lips in astonishment. "He had blond hair like you. But much shorter." Then she knew. "No, it can't be. You... you can't be him."

Tears rolled from his eyes. "Angel."

The name staggered Dawn. She gasped and covered her mouth with her hand, "Angel's a nickname my parents gave me. I haven't been called Angel since I started high school."

The words cracked as Lance said, "Angel, I love you."

Tears of joy fell from Dawn's cheeks. "Tiger?"

Lance nodded through tears of happiness.

Marilyn leaned against Cotton as her eyes, too, filled with tears. Joyce Ann started to cry and buried her face in Brent's chest. A lump formed in Brent's throat. He was so happy for the new couple.

Dawn touched Lance. "Oh Lance, this is a dream come true."

The words were still difficult for Lance. "I know. I'm afraid I'm going to wake up." Dawn threw her arms around him as he squeezed her tenderly.

He whispered again, "Angel."

They clung to each other like they would never let go.

***

The celebration ended all too soon and it was time to return home. This had been an adventure—a miracle, really—the six would never forget, especially Dawn and Lance. With all their things gathered they loaded Brent's van and prepared to leave. But they had lost Walter. He went off with a girl and was already back in Houston.

They hated to end the party but Brent said, "We better get going."

Lance grabbed Dawn. "Wanna ride with me?"

She was excited. "Yes!"

Brent said, "Lance, go to your house first. I want to pick up my board, then I can take Dawn home."

While Dawn hopped on the Honda behind Lance the others piled into Brent's van.

The ride was sweet. They stopped to eat and get fuel. The trip home gave Lance and Dawn some overdue quality time together. On the highway Dawn clung to Lance, still entranced that they had found each other. It was a perfect weekend.

Chapter 27

DEATH AND THE SECRET

This was a dream come true. Lance turned onto Chimney Rock and cruised down the road until he reached Fairdale. A quick right and he was only a short distance from the duplex where he lived with his mother and Bob. Lance was happier than he had ever been in his life with his girl on the back of his bike.

When he pulled into the driveway two cars and an ambulance blocked access on the street. Brent pulled behind Lance and stopped.

Something was wrong, terribly wrong.

Lance's heart sank. "Oh no, my mother!" He bolted from the Honda and ran for the front door.

Dawn knew there was a problem and yelled, "Lance!"

He had already pushed through the door and disappeared. With the ambulance near the front of the house, everyone knew something bad had happened. They all surmised it was Lance's mother. This marked another tragedy in his life.

The others climbed out of the van.

Brent was the first to run up to Dawn. "His mother?"

Worried, Dawn turned to Brent. "I think so."

***

Lance burst into the room. Beverly laid in the bed and Bob sat next to her. Tubes protruded from her nose. Like solemn statues a doctor and nurse stood on the other side of the bed. They reminded Lance of vultures waiting the final moment.

Lance looked at Bob, who shook his head and got up to let Lance take his place. Lance gently grabbed his mother's hand.

Her eyes fluttered open and she peered through Lance with a peaceful smile of recognition. "Timmy."

Tears rolled from Lance's eyes. Her words staggered him, as if he had been hit with a fist. Nothing Jimbo had done hurt as badly as hearing the name of his brother.

He rubbed his mother's hand. "No Mom, its Lance."

Beverly sighed. She appeared happy. "Timmy, you're so big."

The mental pain was almost too much to bear. Bob understood and put a reassuring hand on Lance's shoulder.

"I'm Lance, Mom."

Confused, Beverly said, "Lance?"

"Yes, Mom?"

Again Beverly fairly beamed. "Watch Timmy."

The anguish was too great and Lance barely managed to control his words. There was a secret hidden from everyone, and the secret caused Lance more pain than any physical blow could ever have done. Her words ripped his heart apart.

"I… will… Mom."

"You must take care of Timmy. Promise?" she begged.

"I... " Lance could no longer hold back the tears. " ... promise."

Satisfied and content, Beverly managed a feeble groan and finally let out with a long, slow sigh.

"Bea?" Bob exclaimed frantically.

There was no response. The nurse reached over and felt for a pulse.

Again, Bob pleaded, "Bea?"

"Mom?"

The nurse nodded sadly at the doctor. Her eyes said everything.

The doctor took a deep breath and shook his head. "I'm so sorry."

Bob started to sob. He had always loved Beverly.

Lance was tormented and torn apart inside—the promise! He backed out of the room while mumbling, "No, no!" In shock and disbelief he rushed to the front door where he stopped and paused to look back at the doorway to his mother's room.

"Timmy... Mom, I'm sor… " He cried, "No, no!"

Outside waited Cotton, Marilyn, Dawn, Brent and Joyce Ann. Lance burst from the door. Everyone could see he was in utter agony. Unable to hold back the tears he fell to his knees and sobbed. They watched as he wrapped his arms around his body and rocked back and forth in a torment no one could comprehend or take away. Tears poured down his face. Everyone but Dawn and Brent just stood there. They had no idea what to do.

Brent walked toward Lance to offer his condolences. Dawn ran to Lance's side and wrapped her arms around him to console him in his time of grief.

Lance pulled away. "No, no! Why? Not again." Lance pushed Dawn away and ran to his motorcycle.

She ran after him, "Lance! Lance wait!"

Lance reached his motorcycle and screamed in anguish, "I've gotta get outa here!"

He stood next to his Honda. Dawn was face-to-face with him.

"Lance, I love you. Please don't go."

Through the tears he looked at Dawn. She was what he wanted but the pain was too much. He had broken his promise. "No. Don't love me. I'm no good for you, Dawn. Everyone around me dies!"

Tears rolled down her cheeks. "Lance, I won't die. I want to be with you."

Lance shook his head in misery. "No, no, don't say that. All I can give you is today."

Smiling through the tears, Dawn said, "I'll take that, but I want tomorrow and all the tomorrows I can have with you."

His shoulders drooped. "Dawn, I have no tomorrows. Oh, God, why?"

Dawn touched his arm with both of her hands. "Make your future with me. I love you, Lance. I've always loved you."

Tormented with the death of his mother and his broken promise to her, Lance's body twisted at the memories.

"You don't understand. He died because of me. The bullies from the football team did it and I wasn't there to save him. Timmy killed himself because of what they did to him, and I wasn't there!" Tears rolled down his cheeks. The tormented words continued, "Don't you understand? I promised my mother. She trusted me. You can't trust me—I won't be there. I failed her and my brother and I'll fail you!"

Dawn tried to hug Lance, but he pushed her away. She said, "I know all about Timmy."

He was stunned. "What? You know?" He pulled away and jumped on the motorcycle, sobbing as Dawn tried to hold onto him. He started the Honda against all of her efforts.

She wailed, "Please Lance, don't go."

He agonized over the memories of his broken promise and hesitated. He wanted to stay, but he couldn't. An invisible force pulled him away, but Dawn held him. It was an emotional tug of war as Dawn soothed his distress. He touched her gently on the cheek and she took his hand.

Momentarily at peace he said, "Dawn, you're the only good thing that has ever happened to me. I love… "

Abruptly the demons took over again. "No! Timmy! I promised."

Tortured beyond what any teen could endure, he pulled away.

Dawn continued to sob. "I love you, Lance."

Lance shook his head violently, "No Dawn! Don't say that. They all die!"

Again he pushed her away and Brent managed to grab her as the Honda roared off. Dawn fell to her knees and stared after Lance as the others gathered around her. Marilyn and Joyce Ann knelt down to console her.

She cried, "Oh, Lance, Lance."

The boys stood back from the girls.

Cotton said to Brent, "Man, Lance freaked out."

"Yeah," said Brent.

"Who's Timmy?" Cotton asked.

Brent grimaced, "Timmy was Lance's brother. The jocks on his football team teased him so bad he committed suicide."

"What a bummer."

"That's not the worst part," said Brent, "Timmy slit his wrists with Lance's knife. It's the same knife Lance always carries around."

"Man, that's heavy."

Brent nodded. "It's screwed up."

***

On the highway Lance maneuvered his Honda hard. He drove on the verge of recklessness, pursing a death wish. It was a wonder he could see through watery eyes that stung in the wind. He passed a sign declaring: "San Antonio City Limits."

***

A group of what could now be called Lance's best friends gathered around Dawn and Brent in the Lee School parking lot. Among them were Walter, Ron, Will, Marilyn, Joyce Ann, Marvin, Bill, Mike and many others. They all were concerned and worried.

Dawn asked, "Have any of you heard anything?"

They all shook their heads. "No."

"I called his step-father, went to Surfside, and even Quintana. Nothing," said Brent.

Deeply worried, Dawn tried to concentrate on where to look for him next. Her eyes lit up. "I know where he might be," she turned to Brent, "We must leave right after school."

***

Lance stood near the rope where he had first met Angel and later discovered the secret about Dawn. Tears filled his eyes once more and he flipped the closed knife and caught it. He continued to flip the knife in his hand without looking, each time catching it perfectly. In his mind's eye he saw everything clearly: Angel taking the rope from him, Dawn laughing at him when he met her at the jetty, Dawn and him dancing at the Catacombs, their time at Garner State Park. Again, they were at the rope. Lance saw himself kissing Dawn and remembered her tears as she said, "I love you Lance. Don't leave me." Other visions tortured him as well. His brother Timmy appeared ghostly, pale and lifeless. He glared at Lance and said, "You promised."

Wracked with pain and guilt, he stared at the knife in his hand, bent his head over, and nearly vomited. He mumbled, "I'm sorry, Lord."

***

Dawn ran as fast as she could. Not far behind trailed Cotton, Brent, Marilyn, Walter and Joyce Ann. She reached the rope out of breath and could only stare. Sweet memories of Lance returned to her. Desperate, she checked about in all directions, sure she would find Lance. But she saw no sign of him or any indication he had been there recently.

The others finally caught up as tears filled her eyes. Now they all surrounded the swing. Not far away, campers relaxed around a nearby fire.

"Lance isn't here."

A little boy walked up to the rope. "What's so interesting with that rope?"

Dawn wiped her eyes. "What do you mean?"

"Some crazy guy stood here all day and just stared at it. He never even went in the water," said the little boy

Now all eyes turned to the boy. Dawn held her hand in the air above her head. "Was he about this tall? Blond hair?"

The boy shrugged his shoulders. "I don't remember."

Everybody let out with a groan of frustration.

For a moment the boy showed a bit of excitement. "He did have a neato motorcycle!"

The pendulum of mood swung from desperation to hope.

"At least we know Lance is okay," breathed Dawn.

The little boy remembered something else. "He kept playing with a knife."

Fear and horror filled their faces.

"Oh God, please!" Dawn gasped.

She broke down and wept as Brent tried to comfort her. "Don't worry, Dawn. I know Lance will be okay."

Chapter 28
THE RETURN

Things were a little different. The in-crowd was not as significant as it used to be. There was more of a mixture.

Next to Brent's VW van were Cotton's Chevelle and Dawn's Impala.

Brent had his arm around Joyce Ann's shoulder. Cotton held hands with Marilyn. Around the two couples were Mike, Walter, Bill, Ron, Will and Marvin.

They all listened to Dawn.

"I've heard nothing. How about you, Brent?"

"I've been back to the beach. Nothing. His step-father hasn't heard from him but asked if I'd let him know if we find him," said Brent.

Dawn sighed. "I'll call him if I hear anything. His mother's funeral is tomorrow."

Cotton said, "I'm sure he'll be there."

"I'm so worried about him," said Dawn.

"He'll be okay," said Brent.

Ron changed the discussion. "Our big game against Lamar is tonight. I sure would have liked to see Lance play."

Will Coleman laughed. "Well, we still have Curtis."

Mike rolled his eyes. "We're doomed."

Some chuckled, a few groaned, a few laughed, and even Dawn found herself letting out a giggle.

***

Jim walked up as Dawn took books from her locker. He hesitated, backed up a few steps and said softly, "Dawn."

She turned and automatically backed away.

Jim honestly appeared hurt. "I want to apologize. I've been an arrogant jerk."

Dawn snickered, "Yes, you have. What about Sue?"

"I don't know. She's okay," he said. He shrugged his shoulders. "I just want you to know I see what I've done, and I'm sorry."

"What about Marilyn and Cotton?"

"I just apologized to both of them."

Dawn said, "I love Lance."

Jim didn't appear too happy but he said, "I know and I understand. He deserves you. I hope I have a chance to make it up to him."

Dawn nodded. "Good luck tonight against Lamar."

Jim managed a now-rare smile, "Thanks. We'll need it."

***

On the freeway Lance pushed his Honda. He moved in and out of traffic, but not in a dangerous fashion. He was on a mission.

***

Delmar Stadium was filled to capacity. The game between Lee and Lamar, the two best teams in their zone, would decide the district champion and who would go to the playoffs. This game was a must-win for both teams. The Lee defense was on the field. The Lamar offense came to the line.

The announcer exclaimed, "This is some offensive battle already and we're just in the first quarter. The Lee General's defense is about as effective against the Lamar Redskin's offense as a fishing net holding water! Fourteen to seven, Lamar. If the Generals have any hope of returning to the playoffs, a win here is a must. Right now, they'll need a miracle to pull this one out."

The Lamar quarterback took the snap, set up in the pocket, and threw a perfect spiral for a touchdown over Curtis Sanford.

The first half ended with Lee down less than a touchdown. Coach Turner tried to regroup his players and get the team fired up.

The second half had begun and Lee still needed six to tie. Jim Brown managed to keep Lee within range, but Lamar had the lead and was on offense again within striking distance of another touchdown. That could put the game away and ruin Lee's chances of making it to the playoffs. Again, Lee defensive players set up on the field for the next play. Lamar's offense came to the line.

Frantically Coach Turner signaled a time-out. A slow smile creased his face as he peered intently toward the goal posts.

All eyes turned to follow his gaze. Just what had caught Turner's attention and been so important that he used one of their few remaining timeouts?

A lone football player jogged past the goalposts and in the direction of Coach Turner. He wore the number "43" jersey. The team cheered as Lance ran up the Lee sidelines. As he appeared the change within the Lee team was electric!

Dawn was about to hyperventilate. Joyce Ann and Denise held her up.

From the stands, Brent, Marilyn and Walter created a scene with their impromptu celebration. Brent whistled through his fingers. The cheers from the students who had seen Lance beat Ron turned to a thunderous roar.

Brent screamed, "Yeah Lance!"

"Go Lance!" yelled Walter.

Marilyn asked Brent, "Where did he get number forty-three?"

Brent beamed and nodded as he wiped a tear from his eye. The muscles in his throat tightened and he found it difficult to speak. "His brother wore that number."

Lance ran up to Coach Turner and took off his helmet.

Stern, with a face of stone and his arms folded in front of his chest, Coach Turner said, "What do you want, Renfro?"

"I *want* to play football, Coach Turner," said Lance sincerely.

Coach Turner's expression never changed. "I see." Then he grinned. "Well, it's about time."

Lance held out his hand and opened his fingers to reveal the knife. "Here Coach. I don't need this anymore."

Coach Turner understood, took the knife, and nodded to Lance. Then the coach turned and wiped his eyes, careful not to let the team see his tears.

For a moment, Lance searched for Dawn. He spotted her, waved and gave her a thumbs up. He strolled toward the bench where Jim was the first to greet him.

Jim said, "Lance, I've been a jerk and I'd like to apologize. I'm glad to have you on the team." Jim extended his hand in friendship.

The team gathered around to see what the outcome would be.

Lance took the offered hand and shook it firmly. "Thanks… Jim."

The team cheered!

Jim was curious, "Can you win the game for us?"

Lance shook his head, "No." With a sly grin he added, "But I can get you the ball. You can win the game."

Coach Turner interrupted the two boys. "Renfro, where do you think you're going?"

Confused, Lance turned around toward Turner.

Turner waved toward the football field, "We need you on the field." He grinned, "Can you play free safety?"

Lance started to put his helmet on when Dawn grabbed him and gave his a hug.

Turning to the defense still on the field Turner yelled, "Curtis, get off the field!"

Abruptly Curtis ran to the sidelines and appeared relieved his playing stint was over.

Dawn clung to Lance's arm. "Oh Lance, I was so worried about you."

As they embraced Lance said, "You never need to worry again. Not today or tomorrow or all the tomorrows we have."

Tears of joy filled her eyes. "I love you, Lance."

"I've always loved you, Dawn."

Coach Turner yelled, "Hurry up Renfro, or you're gonna get us a penalty."

"Okay Coach." He gazed back at Dawn and sighed, then bent to one knee and bowed his head in prayer. "Thank you Lord for everything you've given me." Lance jumped up and as he ran onto the field his mother's favorite song floated into his head. As he assumed the position of free safely, he remembered the lyrics, *Que sera, sera. Whatever will be will be, the future's not ours to see, que sera, sera.* He was home again.

Jim, Cotton, Will, Mike, Bill and Ron stood up and started to put on their helmets.

From the bench, a player eyed Jim and the others and snickered, "What are you doing?"

Jim grunted. "Getting ready to go in on offense."

"Are you crazy? Lamar has the ball, not us."

"Not for long," snipped Cotton.

The team began to laugh. They knew.

Lamar came to the line confident and cocky. It was obvious they intended to test the new free safety.

Even the announcer knew what the next play would be. "This will be an easy play. If I was the Redskin quarterback, the first thing I'd do is test this green free safety."

In the stands Brent and Walter turned knowing smiles on each other.

Walter said, "If Mister Hyde is out there, Lamar is screwed."

Brent laughed, "Don't you know it." He cupped his hands and yelled as loud as he could, "Go ahead, test Lance."

Dawn yelled, "Go Lance! Do it!"

The Lamar quarterback dropped back and threw the ball. The receiver ran deep and jumped for the ball, but Lance jumped with him and managed to get position. Just the slightest touch, a few fingers, was all he needed. Lance pulled it in just before he crashed onto the turf. He jumped up and tossed the ball to the referee, who signaled interception. "Lee's ball!"

From the Lee sidelines the team went crazy! The fans roared!

Excited, the cheerleaders jumped all around except for Dawn, who watched Lance's every move. Her heart raced and her eyes remained misty.

Jim Brown turned to the player who had doubted him. "Well, what you waiting for? We have the ball. You better hurry." He laughed and ran on the field.

Everyone in the Lee stands rose to their feet and cheered for Lance and the team. The excitement was contagious but none were more excited than Brent, Walter and Marilyn.

Lance ran straight for Dawn, taking off his helmet as he ran. She ran toward him. He dropped his helmet at the sidelines and they took each other's hands, flashed smiles of contentment, and enjoyed the moment.

Joyce Ann watched and a tear rolled from her eye. "Kiss her, you big jerk!"

Lance pulled Dawn into his arms and kissed her as if there would be no tomorrow. Clinging to each other they spun about in a joyous circle of hope and life.

Remember the first time you fell in love? With faith, anything is possible.

Epilog

Lance was my best friend. Our senior year was great. I'll never forget it. We had some wild adventures, did crazy things, and somehow managed to stay out of jail during our final year of high school. I had more fun with Lance than I've had in the rest of my life.

We made it all the way to the state championship. Lance made an interception that should have ended the game and preserved our five-point lead, but for some reason Jim Brown said he wanted to teach the other team a lesson. He threw a pass and not only did they intercept, they ran it in for a touchdown and stole the high school championship. It was the only time Jim had been intercepted in two years, other than Lance. I don't think Jim ever got over it.

Bill Martin and Mike McClain became teachers and specialized in counseling teenagers against violence.

Oh, remember Billy Gibbons? He went on to form the group ZZ Top.

Gibbons, William Frederick

Many things happened that year. A heavyweight boxer named Cassius Clay came to our school. That summer he was found guilty of draft evasion. He was still one awesome fighter.

During the summer Marilyn got pregnant. She was really afraid of what her family would do to her. Lance came up with a solution and Cotton didn't hesitate for a moment. Dawn helped set everything up, and with the help of Joyce Ann the six of us went on the wildest escapade of our lives. We drove down to Reynosa, Mexico to get Cotton and Marilyn married. There were a few complications, and we ended up in a town called Estaction Ramirez about fifty miles inside of Mexico. It wasn't long before we found a priest and the marriage between Cotton and Marilyn took place in a jail around the midnight hour. It was the only place with electricity and the Catholic priest said he could conduct the ceremony safely there. The wedding was beautiful. The stories we accumulated during and after that trip and the memories we created are ones that have been cherished and retold countless times. Cotton and Marilyn are still together after all these years. Everything worked out great for them, a blessing in disguise.

Jim did marry Sue King, but a few years later they divorced. At the twenty-year reunion I hardly recognized him. Jim was bald and overweight. He would have made a great Santa Clause, but it wasn't Christmas.

I married Joyce Ann. We moved to Bartlesville, Oklahoma where I took over my father's auto repair. We had a boy and a girl. I named the boy Lance. I still see Lance Renfro from time to time.

About fifteen years after we graduated some of us got together. Lance organized it and even made T-shirts. We called the team "Yesterday's Heroes." I even went to Houston a few times to play. It was great to be with them all including Walter, Steve and Pug.

Speaking of the boys, every time I talk on my cell phone, take a picture, or check my email I think about Walter. Lance and I should have listened to the guy. Walter got into the computer business. He ended up with Microsoft. Needless to say, he's wealthy. I think of all the times Lance and I made fun of him, but the joke was on us. All the things Walter predicted eventually came true.

Dawn Alexander was the best thing that ever happened to Lance. Upon graduation from college, he became a veterinarian. They also had one son and one daughter. An opportunity came along to make an investment that would enable them to retire, but they didn't have the money… or so they thought. Remember that comic book about Spiderman that Lance bought the weekend he met Dawn (I mean Angel)?

Well, he tucked it away in his mother's bible, and it turned out the *Amazing Fantasy 15* was worth $250,000. If you don't believe me, just check it out on Google. Lance sold it, invested the money and they made a fortune.

Coach Turner's persistence really helped Lance through those rough stages of adolescence and youth, but Dawn saved his life. Lance and Dawn are still happily together today.

~ Brent Baughman

The Movie

The Gang from '67 (the author far right)

The Author - Senior 1967

AUTHOR'S COMMENTS

Live For Today is based on a true story: mine. Most of the events and relationships in this novel essentially took place. I did, in fact, almost get suspended from school for raising our banner on the opposing school's side at halftime. I did meet a spectacular girl at the swing when I was twelve. My father died when I was ten and my mother told me to protect my younger brother. Although I wanted to beat my brother to a pulp many times, he did not die nor did he commit suicide. There really was a Jim Brown, but he never successfully beat me up. Jim attempted to pulverize me on the sandlot one day, and eventually we became friends. My nickname was "Tiger" and my close family still calls me that today.

The story about the comic book, "Amazing Fantasy 15," happened exactly as it did in the story, but not at Concan. It actually happened in Corpus Christi in a store called Tri-Drive, and is a comic book I still own and cherish to this day.

Live For Today is a combination of events that happened from my sophomore to senior year of high school. The sandlot boys and I did have a confrontation with players from our school's football team in the front yard of Roy Hofheinz's Mansion on Sage Road. Following the altercation, they always let us play football with them. A student in charge of taking pictures for the yearbook came out after hearing about the story and took a picture of our unlikely group. Fifteen years after graduation we formed a flag football team, Yesterday's Heroes. I still have the jersey.

I dated Marilyn in high school. What a beautiful, sweet girl. She had so much to offer, but she committed suicide. I never understood why. I hope this story helps those like her, and in a way it already has. Unlike Lance in the novel, I never did find that remarkable girl at the swing.

Recently, Billy Gibbons reunited with the Moving Sidewalks and is touring in venues around the country. The disc jockey, Russ Knight (also known as the "Weird Beard") did work for KILT. I listened to him all the time. Sadly, he passed away in 2012 at the age of eighty.

Life is filled events that make wonderful stories. Some have historical references that make the story more dynamic and wonderful. Although trends and architecture change or even disappear, they point us back to the glory days of Houston. Take, for instance, eight-track tapes, vinyl records and even cars like the '65 Mustang Cobra, GTO and Stingray. Iconic landmarks like Hofheinz Mansion and the Astrodome (known as the "Eighth Wonder of the World") fill our hearts with nostalgia. After all, even Elvis Presley sang in the Astrodome.

How would you feel if someone tore down the Taj Mahal to build a hotel? What if they demolished the Pyramids to build a huge shopping mall? I feel the same about the Astrodome. Such a vision it was, built by the indomitable Judge Roy Hofheinz. It holds so many wonderful memories for me. I watched cars race about the floor, cheered the Astros, attended many Houston Livestock Show and Rodeos, and even took in basketball games. Yes, basketball. While attending University of Houston in 1968 our basketball team played a pivotal game in the Astrodome. The U of H Cougars and Elvin Hayes took on the unstoppable UCLA Bruins and a guy named Lew Alcindor. Some called it the game of the century… and I was there. It still seems like yesterday. What a battle in the Astrodome! Best of all, my beloved U of H Cougars beat UCLA 71-69!

But by far the most memorable Astrodome event happened when a local radio station arranged for a "Love Ya Blue" surprise welcome for the Oilers. They had just been beaten by the Steelers in Pittsburgh and I was determined to show my support for the season even though they had lost. The welcome back was nothing like what I expected. I honestly thought several totally unrelated functions might be taking place since the parking lot was filled to overflowing.

In I walked to behold a standing room only capacity crowd. The Astrodome was split into halves by the disc jockeys as they anticipated the arrival of the Oilers. One side practiced screaming "Houston" while the other half yelled "Oilers." Back and forth came the thunderous volume of voices, literally a living earthquake that reverberated across the Astrodome. Then the lights were turned out as the players made their way to the stadium. It was dark and still when they pulled in… sixty-thousand plus fans quiet as a mouse. After the players were unloaded the lights flashed on and the Astrodome shook as the fans roared from each side: "Houston" followed with "Oilers!" Dan "Dante" Pastorini and the other Oiler players were in tears.

That was the Astrodome—memories, wonderful and numerous.

But recently another stadium was built next to the Astrodome. This new stadium is just big and expensive, leaving questions that gnaw at my guts: Who in the world decided to build a stadium next to the Astrodome? And who allowed them to do so? What were they thinking? Reliant stadium should have been built at another location, allowing the Astrodome to continue serving the people of Houston and its surrounding areas. Common sense was sorely lacking in those decisions. And now they talk about tearing down "The Eighth Wonder of the World," leaving us with only memories. Ah, but what fond ones they are.

I'm working on a sequel for "Live For Today" and assure you that many of my experiences in the effervescent city of Houston will be included. Yes, Lance, Dawn, Brent and Walter will continue telling their story.

ABOUT THE AUTHOR

The author, Joe Barfield, has led an interesting life, scuba diving, racing cars with his son Beaux Barfield, lifting weights and playing a variety of sports. He met his wife Lucia in Cali, Colombia while on a trip. One time she took him on a trip in the mountains of Colombia and at one point they thought they had entered a guerrilla camp and he would be kidnapped. His first thoughts when he saw their 50 caliber machine guns, "Oh my God I'm going to be kidnapped." To reassure his thoughts, Lucia turned to him and said, "Don't say anything I don't want them to hear your accent." Do you know what he said his next thoughts were? "OH Boy! I'm going to become a bestseller!"

Turns out they were a group of the Colombian military looking for kidnappers. He spent a few days with them and even has a picture of him holding a 50 caliber machine gun with one of the Colombian soldiers. Showing his tenacity, once he was determined to win a Halloween contest and went as far as making an eight-foot monster with moving fingers. He won the contest. For him racing has always been an exciting endeavor, winning his very first race and two years later winning his first professional race at the 6-Hours of Sebring. His son went on to be Race Director for Indy Car. Barfield said there were as many adventures off the track as there were on. A quote from Jim Fitzgerald sums it all up, "When you do it and do it right it is the greatest turn on in the world.

I began writing racing articles and from there I have done movie reviews for magazines and newsletters. I have won a few short story contests.

My script "The Company" won best script in a Fan Story contest. My short script, "The Company," was one of the top six scripts reviewed by actress Dawn Olivieri from the series "Heroes."

I have completed nine novels and nine scripts in a variety of genres, including; action-adventure, family, teen, thriller, religious, drama, comedy, dark-comedy and science fiction. My best novel; *The Cajun*. My best script; *Live For Today*. My favorite novel is *Moon Shadow* because it started me writing.

Currently I'm working on some uplifting scripts and three novels. One of the novels is called *Secuestro*. I came up with the idea when I met Lucia in Cali, Colombia. It's a story of deception, intrigue, war and love. It shows the Colombian people in the true light I find them to be really, loving, caring and very friendly. Also I've working on a script called *El Norte*. This is based on a true story about two Colombians that walked from Colombia to the United States. It describes their adventures and miss-adventures and the love that develops between them.

I started writing twenty-four years ago and for me writing has solved all the problems I couldn't in real life.

CONNECT WITH ME ONLINE

MY WEBPAGE
http://www.jbarfield.com

AMAZON
https://www.amazon.com/author/joebarfield

SMASHWORDS
https://www.smashwords.com/profile/view/thecajun

FACEBOOK
http://goo.gl/wYB6Lj

Live For Today – Movie Trailer
www.youtube.com/user/LiveForTodaythemovie

Moon Shadow - Book Trailer
http://goo.gl/NSN4Ho

The 60's Slang

In the 60s, as today, young people had a different vocabulary. It drove our parents crazy. These are some of the slang words used back then.

A Gas: A lot of fun.

All show and no go: A car that looked great, but couldn't beat anybody.

Ape: Used with "Go," "Gone," or "Went." To explode or go completely berserk.

Bad: Awesome.

Badass: A tough guy. Or a "tuff" guy. A guy you really don't want to mess with.

Bag: To steal, or ask what your problem is. "What's your bag?"

Ball: To have a good time. Also referring to intercourse.

Beat It: Leave the scene in a hurry.

Bird, The: Pointing the middle finger in a vertical position at someone.

Birth control seats: Bucket seats.

Bitchin: Good, exciting, awesome.

Blast: A great time. "We had a blast at the club."

Blew the doors off: Easily beat the other car in a race.

Blitzed: Drunk.

Blown: A car engine with a blower (supercharger) installed.

Blue flamer: Take a big fart... then ignite it with a match.

Bone yard: Auto wrecking yard. Junk yard.

Boogie: To get going.

Book: Leave the scene.

Bookin': Going real fast, usually in a car.

Booze: Alcohol.

Boss: A great or cool thing.

Bread: Money.

Brew or **Brewski**: Beer.

Brody or **Brody out:** To skid in a half circle with the brakes locked up.

Buddha Head: Someone of Asian descent (pre-political correctness).

Bug out: Leave the premises.

Bummed out: Depressed.

Bummer, What a: How depressing.

Burn rubber: To accelerate hard, spinning the tires, making noise, and causing billows of smoke to come from the rear of the vehicle.

Candyass: A real wimp or an uncool thing.

Cat: A guy.

Check it out: Inspect, look over, look at.

Cherry: Pristine, totally clean.

Chick: A girl or a woman.

Chicken, To play: Two cars race toward each other, and the first to pull to the side is the chicken (coward).

Chinese Fire Drill: Stop at a red light. Everyone on the driver's side runs around and gets in on the passenger's side. Everyone on the passenger's side runs around and gets in on the driver's side.

Choice: Really cool or bitchin. "Those are some choice babes."

Chop: To cut down verbally.

Chopped: A section cut out horizontally through the roof pillars of a car to lower the roof.

Chrome Dome: A bald guy.

Church key: Before pop-tops, a beer or soda can was opened with one of these.

"Climb it, Tarzan": An act of defiance said while giving someone "the bird."

Clod: A clumsy or un-coordinated person.

Clue me in: Inform me, tell me. "Clue me in on the story."

Clyde: A person whom one insults or dislikes. A clumsy person.

Cool: Nice.

Cool head: Nice guy.

Cool it: Stop or discontinue. "Here he comes. Cool it, you guys."

Cooties: Someone who wasn't cool had them. No one ever saw them, but you knew who had them.

Copasetic: Very good, all right, no problems.

Cop: Policeman, fuzz, skinner.

Crack up: To laugh hard. To react to something hilarious. "Oh, man you crack me up."

Crash: Go to bed. Go to sleep.

Croak: To die. "You don't have to croak just because he broke up with you."

Crocked: Drunk, intoxicated, boozed, loaded, stoned, plastered.

Cruising: Lee and Lamar students driving up and down Westheimer looking for races, girls, guys, etc.

Crummy: Bad, in bad condition, or unfair. "Look at that crummy surfboard."

Crush: When a boy or a girl liked someone and only his or her friends knew.

Cut it out: Stop, discontinue.

Cut out: To leave without ceremony. "I'm gonna cut out."

Decked out: Dressed up.

Dibs: Most always used with "got." "I got dibs" means whatever you picked first was yours.

Dig it: Do you understand?

Ditz: An Idiot.

Don't flip your wig: See "Don't have a cow."

Don't have a cow: Used when someone was "going ape" or perhaps being a "spaz."

Don't sweat it: Don't worry about it.

Dork: Ding-bat. Not too mentally bright.

Dip: A person one dislikes or insults. Someone of below average intelligence.

Ditch: Leave or miss without a good excuse. To leave or avoid a person. "I'm ditching class today."

Dough: Money, bread, loot. "I need the dough to pay for it."

Down the tubes: In trouble, in bad condition. Also chugging a beer.

Drag: To race another car a short distance

A Drag: Someone or something that's boring or un-enlightening.

Dude: In the 60's, a dude was a geek or a panty waist.

Dumbass: A jerk, dork or someone not too bright.

Easy, Take it: Another way of saying goodbye.

Easy: A girl who was a sure thing sexually.

Fab: Great, fantastic, fabulous.

Far out: Excellent, cool.

Fink: A tattle tale or a rat (jerk). Hence, "He's a Rat Fink."

Five finger discount: Anything obtained by theft.

Flake: A useless person.

Flake off: Get out of here.

Flat top: A very short haircut, usually cut extra close on top.

Flip flops: Thongs for the feet.

Flower child: A Hippie.

Freak out: Temporary loss of control due to an unpleasant event.

Funky: Neat, cool. Also, gone bad. "That smells funky."

Fuzz: The police.

Get or lay rubber: To leave some rubber on the street while accelerating in a vehicle. "He got rubber in all four gears."

Gimme some skin: Shake hands.

Glasspacks: Mufflers packed with fiberglass to muffle the sound. They came in different lengths. The shorter the glasspacks, the louder the car.

Gnarly: Originally a difficult or large wave. "He wiped out on a gnarly wave." Later anything big or difficult

Go all the way: Have sex with.

Going steady: Dating only one special person.

Gone: Cool, groovy, neat, neat. "He's a real gone cat." Or, "I'm gone over him."

Greaser: A guy who used too much grease in his hair. Usually "LB Butch Wax" or "Pomade."

Gremmy: A rookie surfer.

Groovy: Nice, cool, or neat. Used commonly among hippies in the '60s.

Groady: A shortened version of grotesque. A variation: "When we washed the car by hand at the park, we wore our grotees." Also, "That dorm room was so trashed out, it was grotey."

Hacked or hacked off: Angry, disgusted, mad, ticked off, etc. Sometimes used in reference to parents. "My Old Man is really hacked at me about my grades."

Hairy: Out of control. "That was a hairy ride!"

Hangin': Waiting around, taking it easy.

Hang Loose: Relax. Take it easy.

Haulin (ass): See Bookin'.

Hauls ass: A car that really moves.

Heat: The cops.

Heavy: Deep, cool, chaotic, sad, controversial.

Hep, He's: With it. A person who understands the situation.

Hickey: A sucking kiss on the neck that leaves a purple spot.

Hip: Very good. Cool.

Hook: Steal.

Hopped up: See "Souped up."

Hunk: What a girl would call a good-looking guy.

Jacked up: To raise the front end of a car to make it look cool.

Jazzed: Elated, excited.

Keen or keen-o: Someone or something that was cool.

Kipe: To steal.

Kissee: A cross between kiss-ass and sissy.

Kicks: Past time activity done for pleasure. "He gets his kicks by going to the beach."

Knock: Criticize, insult. See Chop.

Knocked up: Pregnant.

Kook: Non-conformist, weirdo.

Later: Goodbye. See you later.

Lay A patch/strip: Spinning the tires and leaving behind rubber on the concrete or asphalt.

Lay it on me: Have someone tell you the story or problem.
Light'em up: Burn rubber.
Lip flappin': Talking about things of little importance.
Loaded: Intoxicated.
Lowered: To drop the suspension on a car all the way around.
Man: An expression of feeling with no real meaning. "Man, that was a wild ride."
Make out: Usually a kissing session in a parked car at a Drive-in or other secluded place.
Meat: A term for "guy" or "man," as in, "Hey Meat."
Midnight auto supply: Car parts obtained through theft.
Moon: To drop your pants, bend over, and show your bare butt.
Neat (neato): Nice, sharp.
Nifty: Meaning "cool."
Old lady or **Old man**: Your parents.
On the make: Usually after a break up of steadies, a guy or girl was "on the make" as they looked hard for a new mate.
Outta sight: Fantastic, awesome. That surfboard is "outta sight."
Pad: Someone's house.
Panty waist: A mama's boy or a geek.
Paper shaker: Pom pom girl.
Passion pit: Drive-in theater.
Peel out: Burn, lay rubber from the tires.
Peepers: Glasses.
PG: Pregnant.
Pig: Cop.
Pig out: Over eat.
Pipe down: Be quiet. "Pipe down, you're in the library."
Pits: The worst. Nasty, bad, awful.
Plastered: Drunk, intoxicated, loaded, crocked, stoned.
Pound: Beat up. "I'm going to pound that punk."
Primo: First class.
Punk: Bothersome person. Clod, Clyde, Melvin. "Don't bother me, you punk!"
Put (someone) **on**: Try to put something over on someone. "You're putting me on?"
Queer: Dorky or dumb.
Rake: To lower the front end of a car.
Race for pinks: Two people race, and the winner gets the other's car.
Rags: Clothes.
Rap: Talk.
Rat Fink: See Fink.
Raunchy: Raw, rank, disgusting.

Retard: A socially inept, dorky person.

Right on: I agree. I concur.

Righteous: Extremely fine, beautiful. For guys, it was generally used when talking about our lives, cars and women.

Riot: Something spectacular. Gas, blast. "It wasn't just good—it was a riot!"

Ripped off: To have something stolen, or to have stolen something.

Rule: To take over. Be the lead.

Sad: An expression of disapproval.

Scarf: To eat very fast.

Score: To obtain something valuable or necessary. "Let's go score some beer." Also, to go all the way with a girl.

Scratch: Money.

Screwed, Got: Cheated out of something.

Screwed up: Made a mistake, messed up in the head, intoxicated.

Sectioned: A section cut horizontally through the body of a car to give it a lower, sleeker look.

Sex pot: A sexy or seductive woman.

Shades: Sunglasses.

Shag Ass: Let's get out of here.

Shake it, don't break it!: Said to a girl who had an awesome wiggle in her walk.

Short: Car.

Shotgun: When a group left a place, someone called "shotgun" and then took the front seat next to the driver against the passenger door.

Skag: An ugly girl.

Skank: Skag.

Skanky: Gross, disgusting.

Skirt: Girl.

Skuzz: Lowdown, undesirable.

Skuzz bucket: An ugly car.

Slut: A promiscuous girl.

Smartass: Someone who is quick and sarcastic.

Smokem': Burn rubber.

So fine: Another cool or bitchin' thing. "He is so fine."

Solid: Something that is okay or all right.

Souped up: A car with an engine modified to go fast.

Spaz: Used as a put down, or to describe someone who was acting retarded.

Split: See Cut out.

Sponge: Everything they get comes from those around them. "Did Bob sponge off you again?"

Square: Someone who was not "cool."

Stacked: Being well endowed. Large breasts.

Steady: Boyfriend or girlfriend.

Stoked: Excited.

Stone: A slow car.

Stoned: Intoxicated.

Stood up: When a guy (or girl) didn't show up for a date

Stuck up: Conceited

Stud: See Hunk.

Submarine races: A place at the beach or PV where couples parked facing the ocean and waited for the Submarines to start racing. Of course, the submarines wouldn't show up, but while you were waiting, you'd make out... for hours, until the insides of your lips were raw.

Swapping spit: Those passionate "get down and really into it," French kisses.

Swordfish fights: See Submarine Races.

Sweat hog: A fat chick.

"T" bucket: A hot rod made from a Model T Ford. A two seater with lots of go.

Teach: A teacher.

The Beach: Surfside.

The Bird: The middle finger.

The Most: Something that is the best or the greatest.

The Man: Police.

Think fast: Get ready, because someone was tossing you something.

Thongs: In the '60s, thongs were something you wore on your feet.

Threads: Clothes.

Three on the tree: A car with a three speed manual transmission and the shifter on the steering column.

Tooling: To cruise or drive around without aim. Example: "We were just tooling around."

Tough or tuff: Neat, cherry, great, bitchin', or even bad. "Wow, she's really a tuff chic!" or, "Sorry, I didn't know. Man, that's tuff."

Trollin': Cruising while looking for girls. Truckin'.

Twitchin': The word used around parents instead of bitchin'.

Wedgie": When someone pulls your underwear up from the back and it ends up in the crack.

Wet willie: A trick played when someone wets their finger and puts it in your ear.

Weeds: Cigarettes, smokes. "Do you have any weeds I can have?"

Weirdo: Nonconformist. An odd, strange, or peculiar person.

What a bum trip: Such a wasted effort or waste of time.

What-say: An expression of greeting. "What-say, man? Long time, no see."

What's your bag, man?: What's your problem?

What's with you?: What's bothering you?

Wheels: Car.

Winner: A person the speaker dislikes. An unattractive, clumsy person.

Wicked: Term of admiration.

Wiggin' out: Going crazy.

Wiped or wipe out: To fall off a wave while surfing, or to crash one's vehicle and severely damage it.

Wiz, Take a: Urinate.

Woody wagon: A wood-sided station wagon.

Zits: Pimples.

SURFER SLANG

Amped: Overdoing it. Excited, stoked.

Anglin': Turning left and/or right on a wave.

Ankle breakers: Small waves.

Avalanche: The white water pouring down the face of a wave.

Awesome: Great, fantastic, outrageous. "Off the Richter" or "Off the Wall."

Back down: To decide not to take off on a wave.

Baggys/baggies: Oversized, loose fitting boxer-type swim trunks.

Bail out: Get away from, jump off, or dive off the surfboard just before a potential wipe out.

Barrel: The breaking motion of a perfect wave. A hollow channel formed inside a good wave when it breaks and curls over.

Beach Bunny: A girl who goes to the beach to watch surfing.

Beached: Totally stuffed from eating.

Beaver tail: A wet suit that features a snap-on crotch, the shape of which resembles a beaver's tail.

Big gun: A surfboard nine-foot or longer especially designed for large waves.

Big surf: Extremely large waves. "Bombora" or "Heavies."

Bitchin: Very good, tops, excellent. "Boss," "Primo," or "Rad."

Blown out: Winds blowing so hard as to chop up the surf and render it unrideable.

Body surfing: Riding the waves without a surfboard.

Bogus: False, lame, ridiculous, unbelievable.

Bombora: An Australian word that refers to a big wave that breaks outside the normal surf line.

Bone yard: The area where the waves break.

Boss: Outstanding, the best. "Bitchin," "Excellent," "Primo," or "Rad."

Breaker: Any wave that breaks on the way to the beach.

Breakwater: A line of large boulders, cement, and/or steel extending out into the water and designed to reduce shoreline erosion.

Bro: Short for "brother."

Bummer - Too bad. A total drag.

Bunny: Beach Bunny

Carve: To make a radical turn. "Hot-Dogging" or "Shred".

Catch a wave: To ride a breaking wave.

Climbing: To carve an S-shaped path on a wave, making a radical.

Dropping: Bottom turn, climbing to the wave's crest, then radically cutting back.

Cheater five: Five toes on the nose. Keep your weight back on the board to maintain trim and speed, squat down and extend one foot forward

Coffin: Riding a surfboard while lying stiffly on one's back with arms crossed.

Crest: The top portion of a wave.

Cruncher: A big, hard-breaking wave that folds over and is almost impossible to ride.

Curl: The portion of the wave that is spilling over and breaking.

Cut back: To turn toward the breaking part of the wave.

Cut out: To pull out of the wave. See "Kick out."

Ding: A hole, crack, dent, or scratch on the surface of a surfboard or car.

Doggers: Multicolored swimming trunks.

Dork: Someone behaving inappropriately. Also see "Geek" or "Kook".

Double spinner: Two consecutive 360-degree body spins on a surfboard.

Drop knee: One foot on the bodyboard, with the other hanging off the back. Difficult and fun.

Dude: A male surfing enthusiast.

Dudette: A female surfing enthusiast.

Dweeb: A geek. Someone who acts or looks like a simpleton.

Eat it: To fall off of a surfboard. Also see "Wipe Out."

El Rollo: Lying prone on a surfboard and holding on to the sides while rolling 360-degrees during a ride.

Excellent: Great, fantastic. exceptional. Also see "Bitchin," "Boss," "Primo," or "Rad."

Face: The unbroken wall, surface, or nearly vertical front of a wave.

Fer sure: The surfer pronunciation of "for sure," meaning absolutely, correct, or definitely.

Geek: Someone behaving inappropriately. Also see "Kook" or "Dork."

Glasshouse: See "Green room."

Glassy: A smooth water surface condition caused by absence of local winds.

Gnarlatious: Anything that's really great or awesome.

Gnarly: Treacherous, large, dangerous. Also see "Bitchin."

Goofy-foot: Riding a surfboard with the right foot forward. Note: Left foot forward is the more common stance.

Green room: The space inside of a tube.

Gremlin: A young hodad or beginning surfer. Also see "Grommet."

Gremmy/Gremmie: See "Hodad."

Grommet: A young hodad. A beginning surfer. Also see "Gremlin."

Ground swell: Large waves generated by distant storms.

Gun: A large surfboard designed for very big waves. Also see "Big Gun."

Hairy: See "Gnarly."

Hang five/ten: To place five (or ten) toes over the nose of the surfboard.

Head dip: Touching the water with your head while surfing.

Headstand: Standing on one's head while riding a wave.

Heavies: Very big waves usually higher than twelve feet.

Hit the surf: To go surfing.

Honker: A really big wave. Also see "Heavies" or "Bombora."

Hot-dogging: Fancy surfing done by a skilled surfer.

Hodad: A non-surfer, usually someone who just hangs around the beach.

Honeys: Female surfers or girlfriends of surfers.

Huarache sandals: Leather sandals worn by surfers with a sole made from tire treads.

Jetty or **jetties**: See "Breakwater."

Kahuna: The Hawaiian god of sun, sand, and surf.

Kamikaze: Riding the board at the nose with arms held straight out to each side.

Kick out: To push down on the tail of a surfboard to lift and turn the nose over the top of the wave.

Knots: Callouses or calcium deposits just below the knee and on the tops of the foot caused by kneeling on the surfboard.

Kook: A surfing beginner. Someone who gets in the way or into trouble because of ignorance or inexperience.

Leash: A cord attaching the surfer's ankle to the surfboard.

Locked in: Firmly set in the curling portion of the wave with water holding down the tail of the board.

Log: Slang for pre-foam board made of wood.

Longboard: A surfboard eight to ten feet long.

Max out: To be over the limit.

Meatball: The yellow flag with a black circle indicating "No Surfing."

Mondo: Something huge. Of epic proportions.

Nailed: To wipe out badly.

Neptune cocktail: The large bellyful of seawater a surfer ingests during a particularly gnarly wipeout. Usually accompanied by the Sand Facial.

Nose: The bow or front end of a surfboard.

Off the Richter" Used to describe something that's very good, excellent, or "off the scale," "awesome," "off the wall," or "outrageous."

Off the wall: Incredible, excellent. "Awesome," "off the Richter," or "outrageous."

Outrageous: Incredible, excellent. "Awesome," "off the Richter," or "off the wall."

Outside break: The area farthest from shore where the waves are breaking.

Over the falls: To wipe out or to get dragged over as the wave breaks.

Pearl: Driving the nose of a surfboard under water to stop or slow down the ride. The term is borrowed from "pearl diving."

Pendleton: A brightly colored plaid wool or flannel shirt worn by some surfers.

Point break: A type of surf break where waves wrap around a promontory of land and curl as they break. A classic example of a point break is located at Rincon, California just south of the Santa Barbara/Ventura County line.

Poser: A surfer "wanna-be." Someone who only dresses the part.

Pounder: A hard-breaking wave.

Prone: Ride with your belly on the board. The most common and easiest way to ride a bodyboard.

Prone out: Pulling out of a wave by dropping to your belly causing the nose to go under water and the tail to turn around.

Primo: The best. "Bitchin," "boss," "excellent," or "rad."

Pull out: To steer a surfboard over or through the back of a wave to end a ride.

Rad/radical: Very good, tops, excellent. "Bitchin," "boss," "primo," or "excellent."

Rails: The rounded edges of the surfboard.

Re-Entry: Attacking the lip, usually going vertically and then turning nose down and re-entering the wave.

Ripping: Executing drastic and radical moves on the wave. Having it your way with a wave.

Sand facial: The result of wiping out and being dragged along the bottom, face-first.

Selling Buicks: The process of reversing the ingestion of the dreaded "Neptune cocktail" or seawater and sand. In other words, puking your guts up. After selling Buicks, it was generally assumed your day at the beach was pretty much over.

Set: A group of waves.

Shape: The configuration or form of a wave.

Shoot the curl: Riding a surfboard through, or in and out of, the hollow part of the wave formed as it crests over.

Shoot the pier: Riding a surfboard in between the pilings of a beachside pier.

Shoot the Tube: See "Shoot the curl."

Shore break: Waves breaking very close to the beach.

Shortboard: Surfboards for small waves.

Shred: To surf aggressively. See "Hot-dogging."

Sidewalk surfing: Skateboarding.

Skeg: The fin at the tail end of a surfboard.

Soup: The foamy part of the broken wave. The white water.

Spin out: The result of a surfboard's skeg and tail end losing contact with the wave face causing the surfer to wipe out.

Spinner: A surfer making a complete 360-degree turn in an upright position while the surfboard keeps going straight. Also called a "360."

Sponger: Somebody who bodyboards.

Stick: Surfboard.

Surfs up: Waves are breaking and surfable.

Stoked: Happy, excited, content.

Stringer: The wood strip running down the center of the board, sometimes used for design.

Surf Bunny: A surfer's girlfriend. A female surfer. Also see "Beach Bunny" or "Dudette."

Surfari: A surfing trip. A hunt for good surf.

Swells: Unbroken waves moving in groups of similar height and frequency.

Tail: The stern or rear end of a surfboard.

Tail slide: Part of a larger maneuver in which the surfer purposely makes his/her fins lose their grip, causing the board to slide.

Takeoff: The start of a ride.

Taking gas: To wipe out.

Tandem: Two people riding on a surfboard at the same time, usually a man and woman.

360: See "Spinner."

Toes on the nose: Riding a surfboard with the toes hanging over the front end. See also "Hang Five/Ten."

Tube: The hollow portion of a wave formed when the crest spills over and makes a tunnel or hollow space in front of the face of the wave. See also the "Green room."

Tubed: Riding inside the "tube."

Walking the board: Walking back and forth on the surfboard to maintain control.

Walking the nose: Moving forward on the board toward the front or nose.

Wax: Substance applied (a wax bar) to the top, or deck, of surfboards for traction.

Wedge, The: A famous, but dangerous, body surfing spot located at the tip of the Balboa peninsula in Newport Beach, California.

Wet suit: A neoprene rubber suit used by surfers to keep warm.

Wipe out: To fall off or be knocked off your board. Also see "Eat It."

Woodie: A station wagon made in the '40s and '50s with wood paneling on the sides.

OTHER BOOKS BY JOE BARFIELD AVAILABLE IN PRINT

AND AS EBOOKS

Link to eBooks:
https://www.smashwords.com/profile/view/thecajun

AMERICA TYRANNY RISING - SERIES

MOON SHADOW THE LEGEND - (Book 1)

MOON SHADOW – (Book 2)
MOON SHADOW'S REVENGE – (Book 3) Available in July

Action-adventure - by Joe Barfield

In 2016 the Muslim Brotherhood has infiltrated America rising in numbers from three million in 2008 to over twelve million in 2016. They have established more than 45 jihadist camps across America determined to take over America and install Sharia law. Members of the Brotherhood attain key spots in the government and military. Hundreds of thousands are granted amnesty, while tens of thousands walk freely across the border of Mexico with the help of America's liberal adminiistration, the Department of Justice and the President of the United States. Unmolested they roam freely across America doing Allah's work. Muslims control the Department of Homeland Security with unlimited weapons and billions of rounds of ammunition. With men in key positions, Christians have been labeled traitors and the debt is given no limit with the express intent of bankrupting America. The United States is destroyed, not so much from outside forces, but rather from the greed within. Unable to pay what remains of the military they simply go home. Along with the President, the Department of Homeland Security and the Muslim Brotherhood control America. The invasion that began in 2008 takes America down. But the Coalition as they call themselves run up against American Civilians armed and deadly. A handful of pilots try desperately to take back America. Against insurmountable odds the future of America depends on its best pilot defeating an F-14 at night but all he has is an antiquated P-51 Mustang and an old Indian Legend; Moon Shadow.

Written in 1996, **Moon Shadow** has become eerily historical with each passing year.

Moon Shadow, the Legend

Considered a traitor and murderer, Beaux Gex, with the help of military friends, is determined to return to America and warn her leaders, but he soon learns they are the problem. Could America's top secret, Aurora Project save or destroy America? Will he be too late? Will the old Indian legend, Moon Shadow, save him or destroy him?

Moon Shadow

Trapped behind enemy lines, a handful of America's best jet pilots, led by ace Beau Gex, discover a dozen old World War II aircraft that they can use in guerrilla-type warfare against the invaders—their enemy. But when the invaders find one of the SR-71 Blackbirds—and intend to use it to destroy the space station, Starburst—Beau and his men are forced to fly one last deadly mission.

Now America's future depends on Beau, its best pilot, defeating an F-14 Tomcat at night. But all he has is an antiquated P-51 Mustang and an old Indian Legend, Moon Shadow.

Moon Shadow's Revenge

America has collapsed but Beau Gex, and Krysti Socorro have found love and they are safe. Their peace is destroyed when Krysti is kidnapped. Beau swears revenge even if he must kill them all to find her. But before he can rescue her it will be a long journey and he will need to deal with the "Crazies," and the Sand People."

For the not-faint-at-heart, *Moon Shadow* begins with one of the edgiest torture scenes since *Marathon Man.* And for those looking for love mixed in with their adventure, *Moon Shadow* satisfies as a tender romance between Beau and Krysti Socorro, an exquisite doctor. Will the betrayal of another tear them apart forever? Can a child save their love or is it too late?

THE CAJUN

(action-adventure) by Joe Barfield

A little Crocodile Dundee and a little Rambo. With a million dollar reward on her head, Kelli Parsons hides in the treacherous Atchafalaya Swamp where living or dying depends on one man--the Cajun!

FORMULA 2000, *the DREAM*

(action – based on a true story) by Joe Barfield

Hoosiers on Wheels.

Keeping a promise, a father enters his son, Shannon Kelly, in the Formula 2000 race series with only a dream and a prayer. When things go from bad to worse it takes a crusty old mechanic, Charlie Pepper, to show them how to win. They soon learn that with Pepper almost anything is possible.

URBAN KILL

(detective thriller) by Joe Barfield

Ex-policemen are taking wealthy men on the hunt of their lives—human prey! The only two witnesses have already been murdered. To solve the case, the lead detective must find a pimp called The Rat and the drug addict Pinky, because they have the answers. But the Rat and Pinky are trying to kill each other. The only people who can help him are a gay bar owner, a hyper, absent-minded forensics expert from India, and his one-eyed, three-legged dog, Lucky.

CHEM STORM

(action – chemical disaster) by Joe Barfield

A reporter and an engineer race to save Houston from a disaster worse than a nuclear explosion—a chemical storm!

Jean Alexander, a reporter for The Houston Post, is young and inquisitive and has gained unauthorized access to an area, where she finds five dead bodies. She wants to know why but a spectator alerts the guards to her presence and she is removed.

The following day a Civil/Chemical Engineer, Travis Selkirk, approaches Jean. She learns he is the spectator from the day before that alerted the guards. He points out the foolishness of her adventure and how the chemicals could have killed her. Jean baits Travis and gets him to agree to show her the dangers that exist on the Houston Ship Channel.

The Company

(thriller, action) by Joe Barfield

No assassin ever walked away from the covert group of the CIA, called "The Compand lived to tell about it. When the last job was botched the assassin walked away and disappeared. The company is afraid the secret mission may be revealed, even after seventeen years. Now they have found the "walker" and a termination team is being assembled. Only one small problem; the mafia also wants the "walker" dead.

WORDS THAT DON'T OFFEND LIBERALS

(Satirical humor) by Joe Barfield

A humorous look at words that don't offend Liberals. The book will probably offend Liberals. This is meant for the entertainment of open minded people. This a book to keep notes. Check it out before you purchase your printed copy. Fun gift for your Liberal friends. They may never forgive you.

PALABRAS QUE NO OFENDEN LIBERALES

(humor satírico) Joe Barfield

Una mirada chistosa en palabras que no ofendan liberales. El libro probablemente ofender a los liberales. Esto es para el entretenimiento de personas de mente abierta. Este es un libro para guardar notas.

Compruébelo usted mismo antes de comprar su copia impresa. Regalo de la diversión para sus amigos liberales. Es posible que nunca perdonará.

The Single Male Parent's Cookbook and Short Stories
by Joe Barfield

The Single Male Parents' Cookbook, is a delightful combination of food and humor, two subjects everyone will enjoy. As a single parent, the author raised his children from the time they were four and six, and soon became an expert in the kitchen. As he said, "My cooking must have been good, because both are adults now and still alive, which only attests to culinary skills... or luck!"

The Single Male Parents' Cookbook combines recipes with humorous anecdotes of things that did and didn't work in the kitchen (and in the author's life). Joe includes lots of fun cooking ideas along with some that were not so good, and even a few you don't ever want to try at home! He shares everything from his Friday Night Special to his Motel Doggy (the electric hotdog). And let's not forget the ROC (Roaches on Chocolate).

Each recipe is followed by a short story about his childhood antics or raising his children. Not everything always ran smoothly. There was that time his boiled eggs blew up all over the ceiling. Oh, and that grease fire… don't ever pour water on a grease fire! But they say experience is the best teacher, and they are right. It wasn't always easy in those years, but Joe managed to retain his sense of humor.

He once heard George Carlin say that although he's over sixty, he never stopped being ten. That describes the author perfectly. In fact, Joe says, "I've been ten six times over, and my life is as fun as ever."

His final comments are, "Are you curious about my recipes for rattlesnake, rabbit, squirrel, and armadillo? I think you'd enjoy the rattlesnake. Can you picture me cooking the Roaches on Chocolate (ROC) on Rachel Ray's show?"

Don't let the cookbook confuse you. Joe is just a normal type of guy. Well, maybe except for the time he got married at midnight in a jail in Mexico. But that has nothing to do with cooking. Neither does the time he almost got kidnapped in the mountains of Colombia when he met his second wife. He's just a wild and crazy guy from Texas.

A Life in Time, My Story – non-fiction

by Joe Barfield

Remember lying on the grass in your front yard and watching the stars? Your best friend was beside you, and neither one of you uttered a word. Then a meteor flashed across the sky and both of you got excited and pointed to the sky.

Our lives are like a flashing meteorite. Often the moments go unnoticed, but we do manage to brighten and touch the lives of those around us. Although we are not all famous or well-known, our stories are important. Each of us has a life in time. These are a series of short stories about my life. From the past comes comparison I'm sure you have heard before, so let me ask you again: Who won the Super Bowl last year? Who won the Indy 500? Who won the last game of the World Series? Who were the Best Actor and Actress at the last Academy Awards? You might remember one, but you probably don't know the others.

Now ask yourself these questions: Do you remember the names of some of your teachers? What teacher helped you in high school? What valuable lessons did your mother and father teach you? And who was your best friend? They may not be famous, but they brightened your life just like that flashing meteorite. I believe life has been an adventure and that we learn from all the things that have happened to us.

The one thing I try to do is look at things in a humorous way. As a child I was called Tiger because I was always into things. I thought I was just curious. As a teenager the death of my father weighed heavily on me. We began to move around. I became angry—a "Rebel," as some of my close friends called me. I had conflicts with religion. When my children were four and six I became a single parent. I learned a lot from them. Most of the stories, I hope, will keep you laughing. There are some that are sad, but that is life. And that is what *A Life in Time* is all about.

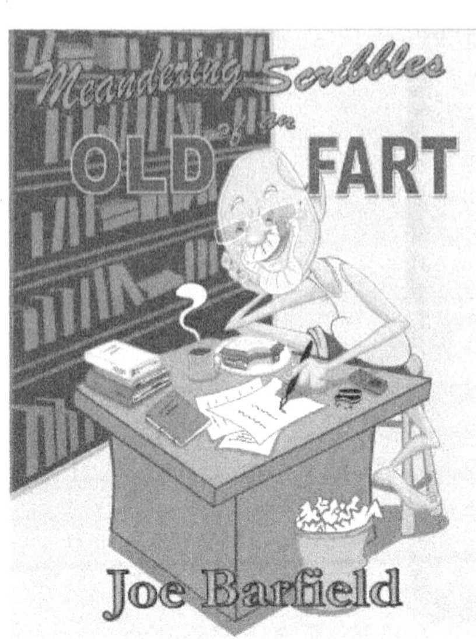

MEANDERING SCRIBBLES OF AN OLD FART – (Political essays) by Joe Barfield

People need to look at their government. I have written articles for over 20 years; from the first Bush to Obama. We have problems we need to face and quit sticking our head in the sand. It's okay to be a liberal or a conservative, but neither exists in our government today. Our politicians do everything but what they were elected to do: Represent the People.

If you are open minded you will enjoy this. If you've only voted one party all of your life then don't download this book. Stop to look at what our politicians are doing today. If you are an open minded Christian you might enjoy this. And if you are you must admit God is probably not too happy. Atheists are offended. Everyone should be offended that they are offended. When talking about being Christian in the military becomes an act of "treason," then we have bigger problems.

America has spent so much time protecting each individual's rights that no one has any rights. Throughout history every great empire has collapsed; there have been no exceptions.

WARNING!

This is for mature audiences so if you're a Democrat or Republican who always voted the same ticket, this is not for you, because it means you are incapable of thinking on your own, so I'd rather you not buy it. If you are a frustrated American upset with the current administrations then you may find these scribbles quit enjoyable.

Should I Forget

A simple reminder, since I might forget. These are scribbles of an Old Fart and you may find repetitions. This is due to "Oldheimers."

DISCLAIMER

Any resemblance to political persons in office is purely intentional.

FOR PETA'S SAKE!

For your peace of mind let it be known that NO animals were injured during the making of these meandering scribbles.

GIVE ME A BREAK!

I'm not a racist, and I'm not a terrorist, I'm just trying to be funny and open your eyes to other solutions. If you have better ideas then you write a book.

FINAL WARNING!

Before you read this I must remind you that you have three choices. You can only pick one so be careful. You are a Democrat, a Republican or an American.

If you picked one of the first two then don't get this book and if you do then don't complain. Americans tell the truth, the other two don't.

Offended yet? You will be; unless you're an American.

FOR OBAMA I'M AMERICA'S BIGGEST THREAT

I'm a white, Christian, heterosexual, and I believe in traditional marriage.

I am America's Biggest Threat.

Get Over It!

3333

A Short Story Collection – fiction

by Joe Barfield

These short stories are based on actual events, and parts from some of my novels, and children's stories. *Sebring, the Rainman* is based on a race my son, Beaux, actually competed. What a race it was!

Night of the Virgin is a combination of events that happened to me in high school. I eventually married her in a jail, in Mexico at midnight. Some of the dialog from *Flight 223* actually occurred. You see I was on flight 223 from Seattle to Houston during the 911 attack. A very strange and chaotic event I will never forget.

I hope you enjoy these as much as I did bringing them to you.

Made in the USA
Middletown, DE
23 December 2023